THE PONY DETECTIVES

Scout and the Mystery of the Marsh Ponies

First published in the UK in 2012 by Templar Publishing,
an imprint of The Templar Company Limited,
The Granary, North Street, Dorking, Surrey, RH4 1DN, UK
www.templarco.co.uk

Cover design by Will Steele
Illustrations by Debbie Clark
Cover photo by Samantha Lamb

First edition

ISBN 978-1-84877-387-5

Printed and bound by CPI Group (UK) Ltd, Croydon, CR0 4YY

THE PONY DETECTIVES

Book Two

Scout and the Mystery of the Marsh Ponies

by Belinda Rapley

For Freddie and Holly B

Rosie and Dancer

Mia and Wish

Alice and Scout

Charlie and Pirate

Chapter One

ALICE cantered into the show ring to a ripple of applause. Her nerves tingled, making her fingers tighten their grip on the reins. Scout, her sturdy Connemara pony, dropped back to trot abruptly. Alice was so rigid that she almost toppled out of the saddle. She tried to relax. She told herself that even though she always got nervous at shows it hadn't stopped her and her dappled grey pony having an amazing summer so far. Doing well in the Fratton Show at the start of the school holidays had set off a winning streak. Since then they'd managed to come first in a class at every show they'd entered; one bedroom wall was starting to disappear behind all the rosettes.

But they'd all been won in straightforward show-jumping classes. Alice knew this was a completely different challenge.

The Eventers Grand Prix was a class she'd never ridden in before, mixing brightly coloured show jumps and natural, more solid cross-country-style fences. The sun was beaming down and she was feeling hot and sticky in a long-sleeved green jumper, rather than her familiar black jacket and tie. The course was against the clock, with penalty seconds added for every knock-down and refusal. That meant Alice couldn't afford to get lost and dither about halfway round. But even though she'd walked the twisting course five times, she was still convinced that she'd forget which way to weave around the tightly packed fences.

"Come on, Alice! You can do this!"

Alice looked up and saw her three best friends – Charlie, Mia and Rosie – waiting by the ropes at the edge of the ring to watch her round. It was Charlie who'd called out, pulling off her riding hat and pushing her elfin-cut dark brown hair out of her large green eyes. She gave Alice the thumbs up. The class was open to horses and ponies of all heights, which meant that the two best friends were competing against each other for once. Charlie had just flown round effortlessly on her 13.2hh speedy bay pony, Pirate. He'd been totally nutty all the way, charging about like a firecracker. But Charlie had just sat quietly, her long legs wrapped around Pirate's sides as she looked for each fence and steered him towards it. She never got nervous in classes and had made it look easy. Pirate had clonked a couple of fences and the poles had come down, but they'd still made a really fast time, putting her in first place.

"Number 224, your bell has rung," a voice suddenly crackled over the tannoy.

Alice shortened her reins. Taking a deep breath, she clicked Scout into a fast canter and circled to the start gates; together they flashed through them. As Scout sailed over the first green-and-red upright,

Alice leaned forward over his withers. His mane brushed her face and she smiled, forgetting all her nerves and the blurred crowd in an instant.

Scout easily cleared fence after fence in the first section of the course – the show jumps – his ears flickering backwards and forwards as Alice slowed him before the uprights and the trickier fences.

Then Alice let Scout open up on the run to the cross-country jumps. He flew over them, ears pricked and stretching out his neck as he galloped across the width of the ring and back again with Alice crouched low over the saddle. For the remaining show jumps she sat upright and steadied Scout again. If she wanted to win, Alice knew she'd have to pull off something special, so as she landed over an upright she turned Scout on the spot inside another fence on her way to the spread. But the grass was slippery, and the dappled grey's near hind skidded from under him, tipping Alice up his neck.

Scout bobbed back up as the crowd 'oohed'

loudly, but he was at a standstill three strides from the fence. Alice instinctively pressed her legs to Scout's side. Her grey picked up and stretched for the back pole to a cheer.

"Good boy!" Alice shouted as they flew over the last jump, and Scout galloped through the finish like a racehorse. Alice stood up in her stirrups and patted Scout's dappled neck, over the moon at completing the tricky course. Scout snorted, shaking his head excitedly as Alice squeezed on the reins to bring him back to a fast trot.

"And that's a clear for number 224," the judge's voice announced. "Scout ridden by Alice Hathaway in a time of one minute thirty-four seconds, which puts her in the lead with three riders to go."

Alice beamed, leaning down to hug Scout as she rode out of the ring. A tall, thin woman with a wide-brimmed hat adjusted a large pair of dark sunglasses as Alice rode past to her friends in the collecting ring.

"That's the last time I give you a pep talk,"

Charlie joked as she slung her arm over Pirate's neck. "You've just beaten my time!"

Alice laughed, sliding out of the saddle and loosening Scout's girth.

"Appreciate your position in first place while it lasts, Alice," Rosie joked with a cheeky smile. She looked like an English rose, with her long flowing yellow hair trailing out from under her hat, her pale skin, round pink cheeks and pale blue eyes. She tucked a stray bit of hair under her hat. "You won't be in the lead for long. I have a feeling that today is Dancer's day."

Rosie flapped her legs against her pony's side. Dancer, her 14.1hh cobby strawberry roan mare, grunted. She was busy stuffing as much grass into her mouth as possible and was not happy about being interrupted. She swished her chestnut-coloured tail and started to slowly make her way down the roped tunnel.

"Good luck!" Alice giggled, as she rubbed Scout's hot neck under his mane and kissed his velveteen muzzle, breathing in his warm pony smell.

"Luck has nothing to do with it," Rosie called over her shoulder as she trotted away in a wonky line. "It's all down to talent. Fortunately, Dancer and I have it in bucketloads. That, and a cunning plan that will get us the fastest time of the day..."

"Honestly, Rosie never takes anything seriously!" Mia tutted as she craned her neck to watch. Wish Me Luck, her beautiful palomino pony, stood next to her, behaving herself impeccably as always. Together they had already competed in their Ridden Show Pony class, which involved Mia and Wish both looking immaculate, Mia in her pink tie with silver dots and Wish in her matching bright pink velvet browband. Wish had walked, trotted and cantered around the ring elegantly, without putting a single well-oiled hoof out of place. As a result, the pretty part-bred arab had a huge red rosette fluttering from her bridle.

The bell rang, and in the ring Rosie pushed

Dancer into a slow, reluctant canter. The mare stepped clumsily over the first fence, then trundled on to the second, dropping back to a trot as she landed. Rosie cantered Dancer steadily past the third fence, a tricky oxer, and made straight for the fourth.

"Rosie!" Charlie and Alice both cried out, waving their arms. "Fence three! You've missed it out!"

Rosie went pink but looked pointedly ahead, not changing course. Dancer cat-leaped the fourth jump before the tannoy suddenly crackled into life.

"Competitor 239, you've missed fence three, which means elimination," the judge called out. Rosie kept up her slow canter all the way out of the ring, looking pinker than ever.

"I had hoped they wouldn't notice," she explained as she pulled up, puffing. "Dancer would never have got over that fence, so I thought I'd just nip round it. I planned to do the same with all the cross-country fences – that way I might have beaten Alice's time. I reckon I'd have got away with it, too, if you lot hadn't made such a fuss!"

As Alice and Charlie looked at each other and laughed at Rosie's crazy plan, Dancer dropped her head to pull at the grass just outside the ring, acting as if she hadn't been fed for weeks. In her summer coat, only her large rump still had the mixture of white and chestnut hairs in it; the rest of her had turned chestnut. Rosie tried to walk Dancer on, but Dancer refused to budge. She stood stuffing as much of the luscious grass down as possible, her large rump totally blocking the narrow entrance into the jumping ring.

A shrill voice called out.

"Could you *please* move that pony out of the way!"

As Rosie attempted to pull up Dancer's head, Charlie, Mia and Alice all let out silent groans. They knew without looking that the high-pitched voice belonged to Tallulah Starr – all glittery eyeshadow, sparkly nail varnish and masses of curly light brown hair. Her dad owned a successful second-hand car sales business and he bought Tallulah anything she asked for. She'd made it well known that she wanted to be a top showjumper, so her dad bought her an ever-changing string of grey ponies (they all had to be colour coordinated) to help fulfil her dream. She also had an ever-changing round of grooms and instructors, the best her dad's money could buy.

The ring steward called out Tallulah's number and she kicked her pretty Connemara cross, Diamond Starr, into a fast canter. As she rode past, the others saw the white writing on the back of her striped green, pink and yellow cross-country colours:

Tallulah Starr & Diamond Starr,
sponsored by Starr Cars,
the classiest motors in town

Tallulah rode up to the start gates. A man dressed in jeans and a flashy, open-necked shirt stood by the edge of the ring cheering loudly: Tallulah's dad. He pointed an expensive-looking video camera at her.

"Come on, Lulu – show 'em who's got Starr quality!" he shouted in a strong cockney accent.

Tallulah posed for the camera, then leaned forward, setting her face and flinging the reins at Diamond Starr as she flapped her legs urgently. The grey pony shot forward in surprise, then settled and jumped each fence cleanly and steadily while Tallulah flung herself about on top, leaning left and right dramatically and squealing "Hup" at the top of her voice in front of each fence. For all his money, the one thing Tallulah's dad couldn't buy his daughter was ability.

Diamond Starr neatly cleared the last fence and flew through the finish line with Tallulah clinging on tightly. She rode back to the exit, looking smug as her dad roared his approval from the edge of the ring. The tannoy crackled, then there was a pause before the judge cleared her throat.

"Well, although that was a clear round for number 265, Tallulah Starr riding Diamond Starr," the judge announced after a pause, "I've just been informed that unfortunately it won't count because you started before the bell went, so that's elimination, I'm afraid."

Tallulah turned crimson and leaped out of the saddle, abandoning Diamond Starr as she ran towards the judge's box at the far side of the ring. Her dad was already on his way. Alice caught hold of Diamond Starr's reins while Charlie loosened her girth and ran up the stirrups. The pony turned her large grey head and blinked her dark, long-lashed eyes sweetly at them.

"Glad of a bit of a fuss, probably," Rosie commented as she patted the mare. "She doesn't get any from Tallulah."

"Her grooms are always running round like

mad so they never have time either," Mia added, rubbing the grey's forehead. Diamond Starr lowered her face and leaned in towards Mia as the last competitor, a young boy, rode past them into the ring. He cantered his flighty chestnut pony in circles while Tallulah held up the proceedings, arguing with the judges before stomping back to them.

"They won't listen," she stormed, snatching her pony's reins as the bell went behind her and the boy finally started his round. "Not that I care. I mean, this class doesn't count anyway. It's not even proper showjumping, is it?"

Behind them in the ring, the young boy and his chestnut pony had refusal after refusal at the third fence, the oxer that Rosie had avoided. The bell sounded again for his elimination.

"That's the end of the class and we have a winner – Scout and Alice Hathaway take first place," the judge boomed over the loudspeaker as the boy walked out looking glum, "with Pirate and Charlotte Hall in second and Blue Bandit in third with Hannah Edge. Would the riders and their ponies make their way back to the ring for the prize-giving."

Tallulah was about to drag Diamond Starr away during the lap of honour when Poppy Brookes appeared through the crowds, making a beeline for Mia and Rosie. Poppy was like a local celebrity on the circuit because she was the best showjumper in the area with her piebald ace, Moonlight. The Pony Detectives all looked up to her and were delighted that she'd started to say hello to them ever since Moonlight had been stolen earlier in the summer and they'd helped to track him down. After the four friends had successfully solved the mystery, they had decided to call themselves the Pony Detectives, and each of them was hoping for a new case to investigate soon. Mia waved at Poppy excitedly. Tallulah caught the look on Mia's face and tutted.

"I don't get the big deal about Poppy Brookes.

I mean, I'd be way better than her if I could *just* get my hands on the right pony," Tallulah boasted dismissively.

"Really?" Rosie exclaimed, thinking that Tallulah couldn't actually believe what she'd just said. After all, it was clear to everyone that Poppy and Moonlight were in a class of their own. Since winning the Fratton Cup they'd taken on bigger horses in huge jumping classes; the pair had won most of them, too. That was more than could be said for Tallulah, who pushed and pulled her honest, talented mounts around courses that were too big for her, if not for the ponies she rode.

"Oh, yes," Tallulah sniffed importantly, fluttering her glittery lashes for a moment. "I keep trying to get hold of top-class jumpers so that I can finally beat her, but I haven't had any luck yet. Dad's made loads of huge offers at shows whenever a pony does really well, but no one's agreed to sell their ponies to me yet – I can't think why."

"I can," Rosie whispered to Mia. "*Everyone* knows that Tallulah's got a habit of ruining good ponies by jumping them over fences that are too big."

"And once she's spoilt them," Mia whispered back, "she thinks they're useless and sells them like they're one of her dad's second-hand cars."

"What was that?" Tallulah asked as the girls exchanged looks.

"Oh, nothing," Rosie said quickly.

"It's odd, isn't it?" Tallulah sighed, carrying on. "Dad even offered to buy Moonlight once. To be honest, he wouldn't really go with my colour scheme of all greys. But Poppy Brookes said she wouldn't ever sell him at any price, anyway. So I'm still searching for a pony who can take him on. And I *will* find one, especially with the money Dad can afford to pay. Then it'll be me that everyone gets excited about talking to at shows, not Poppy."

Tallulah fell silent as Poppy reached the group,

which was soon joined by Alice and Charlie who rode out of the ring with their red and blue rosettes fixed to their bridles.

"Congratulations, you two," Poppy beamed up at them. Alice went slightly pink, still a little bit in awe of Poppy. Charlie flung herself out of the saddle. Tallulah loitered nearby, eavesdropping as she bent down pretending to fuss over the tendon boots wrapped around Diamond Starr's front legs.

"Scout picking up first prize is starting to get a bit of a habit these days. Moonlight, you'll have some serious competition if he carries on like this!" Poppy smiled, stroking her pony's black and white neck. "If I didn't have you, I'd love to ride Scout. He's a real star, isn't he? Alice, please tell me you're not thinking of entering the Sweetbriar Stud Cup next weekend? That's one I wanted to win..."

"You never know," Alice laughed, well aware that Poppy was joking. She'd watched the

Sweetbriar Stud Cup the year before. It was held at the last show of the summer holidays and the fences were massive; there was no way she'd even get over the first! The Fratton Cup was pretty much as big as she wanted to jump on Scout without denting his confidence, or hers. For Moonlight and Poppy, though, the Fratton Cup had just been a warm-up on the way to much bigger classes. Since that show, Poppy and Alice had hardly competed against each other.

Poppy smiled, then looked over to the ring. "Right, my class is on next, so I'd better get going. Lovely to see you all!"

She jumped lightly into the saddle and trotted Moonlight off to the warm-up area, waving over her shoulder.

As Poppy disappeared Alice noticed Tallulah standing on tiptoes, peering over the top of Diamond Starr's saddle to get a better look at Scout. A second later her dad walked over, looking ruddy-faced after continuing his row with the judges. Tallulah whispered something to him. The next second, he pulled out a cheque book and marched towards Rosie.

"Right, how much do you want for this nag?" he boomed, nodding towards the sleepy roan mare in front of him.

"Not that one, Dad!" Tallulah shouted rudely, pointing wildly towards Scout. "It's the *grey* pony Poppy said could beat her in the Stud Cup!"

Mr Starr turned to Alice and repeated his question to her, sizing up Scout like he was a shiny new sports car. Alice felt half as if she was about to laugh out loud at Mr Starr and half furious that Tallulah had even got him to ask the question.

"He's not for sale," she told him, shaking her head in amazement. "He belongs to Mrs Valentine, but there's no way she'd ever sell him. She put him on permanent loan to me a year ago."

"What? He's not even yours?" Tallulah butted in, dragging Diamond Starr towards Alice irritably.

"It doesn't matter, princess," Mr Starr said, ignoring Alice and waving his cheque book about. "We'll just have to find this Mrs Valentine, then persuade her to change her mind."

Tallulah squealed, hugging her dad before they rushed back to their box, where one of her grooms already had a different pony waiting for her to ride in the next class against Poppy.

Chapter Two

"HONESTLY, what part of 'permanent' does Tallulah not understand?" Charlie laughed.

"I can't believe she'd even get her dad to ask!" Mia agreed.

"Tallulah wouldn't have looked twice at Scout when I first got him, either," Alice said. "He was so scraggly and unloved. Only now he's doing brilliantly and Poppy's being nice about him, suddenly she's interested!"

Alice leaned forward and hugged her grey pony. She'd first caught sight of Scout when she was cycling along the path next to Dragonfly Marsh. It was a shortcut from her home to Rockland Riding School, where she used to help out at weekends and where Charlie and Mia had kept their ponies before Rosie's parents inherited Blackberry Farm. The grey pony had peeped nervously through the grass. He had been a bit thin, with slightly overgrown hooves, and his coat was ungroomed. His tattered headcollar was held together with baler twine and his tail dragged through the marsh grass. Alice had fallen in love with the lonely little pony at first sight.

Pretty quickly she'd started making special trips each day after school to see him, taking apples and carrots. He'd stood waiting for her and whickered when she turned up. She spent longer and longer sitting on the fence, keeping him company as he grazed nearby, pretending that he was hers. Secretly, she dreamed that one day he just might be. She'd been desperate to find out who, if anyone, owned him.

"Are you coming or not, Alice? I need an ice cream before I melt," Rosie declared. Alice realised that she'd been daydreaming and that the others were all staring at her, waiting for her reply. She nodded, and together they started to make their way through the crowds towards the food stalls.

Alice wandered along, Scout by her side gently nuzzling her arm. She smiled as she remembered the magical day the advert had appeared in *Pony Mad*: 'Dappled grey pony for loan owing to sad circumstances. In need of love and attention. Currently turned out on marshland on the Suffolk coast.' Alice had persuaded her parents to call the number, just in case it was the same pony she'd fallen in love with on Dragonfly Marsh. To her absolute delight, it was. So Alice and her parents had met the pony's owner, a Mrs Valentine, at the marsh. Mrs Valentine had explained that she'd had Scout since he was a foal for her daughter, Scarlett. But Scarlett wasn't well, and Mrs Valentine couldn't look after both Scout and Scarlett. She couldn't bring herself to ever sell her daughter's pony either, though, so a permanent loan seemed the best solution. Alice's parents had agreed to it there and then, seeing how deliriously happy it made Alice. Just a few weeks after Rosie's family inherited Blackberry Farm, Alice excitedly led Scout into his new stable there.

She bought an ice cream and sat on the grass with the others in the shade of a tall beech tree. The four ponies grazed at the end of their reins as the girls watched Poppy beat the opposition and take her class easily. Tallulah and one of her other greys, Starr Dream, came fifth.

"I guess we'd better get the ponies back to the farm," Charlie said, scratching behind Pirate's ear then tightening his girth, although Dancer made it clear that she quite liked the sweet grass under the tree and wasn't that keen to go anywhere.

When she finally raised her head they hopped into their saddles and rode together through the dusty lorry park, towards the exit. They were just a few strides away when a tall, thin woman dressed smartly all in green, with a big hat, blonde hair and huge sunglasses, stepped into their path.

"Alice...?" she asked softly, smiling as she tipped her glasses down just enough to look over the top. "Alice Hathaway?"

Alice stopped for a second, staring hard as her eyes widened. It had been over a year since she'd last seen the woman standing in front of her, but she hadn't changed a bit.

"Mrs Valentine!" she beamed. She sat up taller in an instant, more pleased than ever that Scout had a red rosette flowing from his bridle. That way Mrs Valentine could see at once how well he was doing and how well she was looking after Scarlett's pony.

"You remembered, how sweet," the woman said warmly in a voice like honey. "I thought I might catch you here. I'd been hearing very good things about this pony so I decided to come and see for myself. He was certainly very impressive earlier."

Alice nodded, smiling back.

"I thought I'd take some pictures of him,"

Mrs Valentine purred, patting her camera. "You know, to show Scarlett. She wanted to come today but she couldn't; she's still too ill, you see. This is the next best thing. So if you could jump off, get the pony standing nicely square, that's it. Scarlett will be so happy to see Sunny... "

As Alice slid out of the saddle she felt her knees suddenly buckle. She hadn't heard Scout called Sunny for over a year and it was a sharp reminder that he wasn't really hers. But there was no reason for Mrs Valentine to remember the new name that Alice had given Scarlett's pony, even though she'd written to tell her. Alice had started calling Scout by that name right from when she'd first seen him on Dragonfly Marsh and he'd trotted into view through the long marsh grasses like a lone adventurer. When she'd found out from Mrs Valentine that his name was Sunny she'd tried using it, but Sunny just hadn't suited the grey pony at all – it was more of a chestnut kind of name, and Scout had never responded to it anyway.

Alice gently pushed Scout back a step so that he was standing almost square, with his front and back hooves in line, then she stood by his head smiling happily at the camera and making sure that his rosette was on full display.

Mrs Valentine's finger hovered above the button. She paused and looked over the camera.

"Hmm, the picture doesn't look quite right somehow. I know, why don't you take one step away from the pony, Alice," she said, smiling encouragingly. "That might be better..."

Alice apologised, suddenly feeling awkward, and quickly moved backwards. Scout took a step towards her. Alice laughed. A tinkly laugh came from Mrs Valentine as she waved Alice to the side once more. Alice set Scout up again then took a tentative step back. Scout stretched out his nose towards her, then heard a horse neigh in the distance and raised his head, his ears pricked, looking handsome.

Mrs Valentine clicked away frantically then

held her hand up to the camera to check the last frame. Her face creased into a smile.

"Excellent!" she announced, looking very pleased as she packed her camera away. "The advert in *Pony Mad* will look perfect."

"Advert? What advert?" Alice said, wondering what Mrs Valentine was going on about. "What for?"

"Oh, I'm sorry, didn't I say?" Mrs Valentine said breezily. "I'm putting Sunny here up for sale."

Chapter Three

ALICE'S insides turned to ice and she felt light-headed as she stood in the midday heat.

"But... but I don't get it," she stuttered, looking desperately round at the others. "You've had Scout since he was a foal – you said that you and Scarlett would *never* sell him, that I could have him on permanent loan..."

"Did I? Oh dear. Well, well, things change, don't they?" Mrs Valentine said smoothly. "You see, Scarlett's lost all interest in ponies now so I've decided that it's time to get rid of him. Obviously, you'll have first refusal before the advert comes out because I'm sure you're so attached you couldn't bear to part with him. That's only fair now, isn't it?"

She smiled at Alice encouragingly. Alice nodded, breaking into a smile too as she felt relief flood through her. As she started to breathe again, her heart crashed against her ribs. She knew that her parents didn't have much money at all, but if the price wasn't too high she might be able to help raise some of the cash herself.

"How much are you asking?" She could hardly believe that she was actually saying the words. The dream of owning Scout suddenly felt as if it might finally come true – he might become her very own pony at last! Her mind raced. She remembered how sorry and neglected Scout had looked when she'd taken him on loan and hoped it would be a price she could afford. She barely breathed as Mrs Valentine lowered her glasses a fraction and gave Scout one final appraising look.

"I'll tell you what, as you've looked after him for a year, I'll do you a deal," Mrs Valentine said, wrinkling her nose in a smile at Alice, "at £6,000.

After all, a pony with as many wins as this one is *very* valuable."

Alice gasped. It felt as if all the wind had been knocked out of her at once. For a second the field in front of her spun and she leaned heavily against Scout, tangling her fingers in his mane. There was no way her parents could even *begin* to afford that much – she didn't even have to ask. They never said anything to her, but she knew that sometimes they struggled even to find the money to keep Scout at Blackberry Farm each month, let alone buy his hard feed and his hay as well as pay to have him wormed, his hoofs shod and his teeth checked. To save up the figure Mrs Valentine wanted would take for ever, even if she helped like mad. It was impossible.

"Hang on a second, though," Mia suddenly piped up after the initial shock of Mrs Valentine naming such a huge price. "Scout wasn't worth anywhere *near* that much when Alice first took him on!"

"Mia's right!" Charlie agreed crossly. "Alice has put in all the hard work!"

"Exactly! It's totally unfair!" Rosie added, going pink with indignation.

Mrs Valentine turned her sunglassed gaze in their direction.

"I *have* dropped the price for Alice, not that I see it has anything to do with *you three*." She bristled just for a second, then forced a bright smile onto her face as she looked pointedly back towards Alice. "Now, the price isn't up for negotiation. Would you like to buy him? You do realise, don't you, that if you don't there'll be plenty who will. In fact, I wouldn't be surprised if he's bought by the first person to see him."

Scout stood quietly beside Alice, his warm breath on her face. She rested a shaky hand on his neck.

"I... I can't afford him," Alice said, dropping her head as the grass in front of her started to blur.

Mrs Valentine arched an immaculately

groomed eyebrow over her dark glasses.

"Oh, now, that *is* a shame," she said in a sympathetic voice, "but I won't prolong your agony. The advert goes into the next issue of *Pony Mad*. He'll be snapped up in no time."

Alice was still shaking long after Mrs Valentine had disappeared back into the crowd at the showground, her wide-brimmed hat bobbing out of view. She hadn't gone without asking Alice where she kept Scout. Alice had nearly lied, but anyone local would know where she lived, anyway. She was too stunned to properly take in what had just happened, as around her Mia, Rosie and Charlie all spoke over each other. Alice hugged Scout, then climbed into the saddle feeling numb.

"I thought you had an official loan agreement? I don't think she can do this if you have!" Mia said crossly as they rode out of the showground and headed along the bridleways towards Blackberry Farm.

"She promised she'd send one," Alice explained quietly, "but it never turned up. Mum tried to ring her loads of times but she never answered the phone. We didn't want to bother her too much because we reckoned she must be busy with Scarlett. I wrote to her once, but she didn't reply..."

Alice trailed off. After a while she'd stopped worrying about the loan agreement not turning up. After all, permanent meant for ever – at least, that's what she'd always thought. Until now.

"We can't just let her turn up like a whirlwind out of nowhere and put Scout up for sale," Charlie ranted, "not after Alice has done so much with him."

"And he loves it at Blackberry Farm – it wouldn't be the same without him!" Rosie agreed. "We *have* to do something!"

"Clearly," Mia said, "but it'll have to be really

quick… I think this might be a case for the Pony Detectives!"

"I think you're right," Charlie agreed.

"Totally," Rosie added.

They'd all been excited about finding a new mystery to solve, but a mystery involving one of their own ponies really raised the stakes. They couldn't afford to fail.

They fell silent as they concentrated, walking their ponies through the woods on a long rein. Alice knew they were up against it, but her mind had gone totally blank. She leaned down and hugged Scout, her arms around his solid neck as he walked along slightly uncertainly, his ears flickering backwards, sensing that something was wrong.

"I know!" Mia suddenly cried. Alice looked up at her, eyes bright with expectation. "I think the first thing we should do is try to change Mrs Valentine's mind."

"And how exactly do we do that?" Rosie asked,

looking confused. "She seemed one hundred per cent determined about selling Scout."

"She might be, but Scout isn't Mrs Valentine's pony, remember?" Mia said, starting to get excited as she spoke. "Scout was Scarlett's pony, and she can't be much older than us. I know she's lost interest in ponies, but she might be able to help us persuade Mrs Valentine not to sell Scout if we can show her how much Alice loves him."

"Yes! And Scarlett's had him from a foal," Charlie said, "so she must still have a soft spot for him. It *has* to be worth a shot."

"But what if Scarlett falls in love with him all over again and decides to keep him for herself?" Alice said, starting to panic as she imagined the reunion and convincing herself that she would lose Scout either way.

"That's a risk we'll have to take," Mia said grimly.

Alice sighed then nodded, knowing Mia was right.

They started to make a plan, deciding to pay Mrs Valentine and Scarlett a visit the next morning. They turned off Duck Lane between a gap in the overgrown hedges, then rode along the rutted track that led to Blackberry Farm's wooden, slightly wonky gate. Rosie jumped off and hauled the gate open, waiting while the others clattered onto the small square concrete yard. The girls had stabled their ponies together there since Rosie's parents had inherited the farm the year before. There were eight stables in total in the yard, but they only used four. The others had been converted into a tack room, a feed room and a stable for keeping wheelbarrows, forks and brooms in, with one spare. The girls looked after everything, which Rosie's mum, an artist, had insisted on from the start. For the girls, it was pony heaven.

The assortment of chickens in the yard squawked and scattered. They regrouped just as Beanie, Rosie's brown and white patched Jack Russell, flew out of the cottage, barking his greeting and sending the chickens flapping off again in every direction. Alice looked round at the little yard that was Scout's home, almost hers during the time she wasn't at school. She felt numb at the thought of him not being there.

"Do you know where Mrs Valentine lives?" Charlie asked.

Alice nodded.

"It's 13 Hollow Hill," she said quietly. "I remember from when I got Scout last year, Mrs Valentine wrote it down for us when Mum and Dad insisted on having contact details in case anything ever happened. We didn't meet her there, though – we only met her at Dragonfly Marsh."

"We've got a map," Mia said as they tied up their ponies in the afternoon sun of the little yard. The Pony Detectives had used the map to find Hawthorn Farm, Poppy's yard, when they were searching for clues over Moonlight's disappearance earlier in the summer. "We can find it on that."

The ponies stood quietly, pulling at the haynets which the girls had left up from before they'd ridden to the show that morning. It seemed like a lifetime ago, and as Alice untacked Scout with a heavy heart she wished more than anything that she could go back in time: then she could decide not to go to the show. That way she would never have bumped into Mrs Valentine.

Alice wanted to gallop over to Hollow Hill straightaway so that she could find out as soon as possible whether Scout would be safe. But she knew the others were right – it was too late, and the ponies had done too much that day to go out again. As she headed back to Scout with her hoof pick and sponge and a bucket of warm water, she felt the twist in her stomach again. Scout turned his head to look at her as she walked across the yard towards him, his big trusting eyes watching her quietly.

As Alice leaned down by Scout's near fore he automatically lifted his leg, nuzzling her back while she picked out his hoof. She went round all four, patting him after each one. Then she sponged down his neck, back and where his girth had gone. She knew that he could tell something was wrong as he watched her, nudging her arm every now and again.

"I won't let it happen," Alice whispered, resting her forehead against his. Alice's eyes welled up as she felt Scout's warm breath. She tried to swallow the lump in her throat as he sighed heavily, blinking and shifting his weight. The possibility that one day, very soon, her pony might not be around made her heart break. Along with the three girls, Scout was her best friend and she didn't know what she'd do without him.

Alice left him and trooped back with the others to the feed room. The comforting smell of sweet molasses rose up as they opened the feed bins and dug their scoops into the pony nuts and chaff, dropping the contents into their ponies' bowls. While the other three noisily planned the trip the next day, their voices seemed to fade into the distance as Alice listened to the ponies whickering softly in the yard. Dancer scraped her hoof, her metallic shoe ringing out impatiently as it sparked against the concrete.

Alice ladled a scoop of pony nuts into Scout's well-worn feed bucket, and she knew that there was no way she could face the world without him in it. She dipped her scoop back into the bin, bringing it out with shaking hands, and seeing the bucket blur as she looked at it. Suddenly, the numbness inside fell away and her breath started to come in jagged sobs. Rosie dropped Dancer's bucket and put her arm around her, and Alice felt herself crumble as the reality finally hit her.

"We'll stop Mrs Valentine selling him, Alice," Mia said, and she and Charlie put their arms around her too. "We're proper, official Pony Detectives now, remember? We can do this!"

"We'll stop at nothing!" Rosie agreed.

"This'll be the easiest problem in the world to

solve," Charlie added optimistically. "Once we've seen Scarlett tomorrow, everything will be sorted."

"Exactly," Rosie said, hugging Alice tighter. "Now the Pony Detectives are on the case, Mrs Valentine doesn't stand a chance."

Alice sniffed, her head drooping. She knew how lucky she was to have her three best friends with her; she just hoped more than anything that they were right.

Chapter Four

The girls met at Blackberry Farm earlier than usual the next day, when the sun was bright but it was still slightly chilly. They raced to the paddock and rode their ponies bareback up the path to the yard. They mixed feeds and flicked the ponies over, then gathered in the tack room. Mia pulled the map which they'd used earlier in the summer from her pocket.

"There's Dragonfly Marsh," Alice said, finding it a couple of miles away from Blackberry Farm, across fields and down little lanes.

"And look, there's Hollow Hill, way over there," Charlie pointed out, leaning over Alice's shoulder. Alice traced the route between Hollow Hill and Dragonfly Marsh with her finger. The map clearly showed that the two places were separated by fields, hills, woods and farms, all interlaced with lots of bridleways and lanes.

While Mia worked out the route, Alice turned her mind to more important things than where places were located on a map. She picked up her grooming kit, and as she gently brushed Scout's face she ran through what she would say to Scarlett. Scout lowered his head, closing his eyes. Alice smiled and kissed his forehead, then felt her heart squeeze hard as she remembered that very soon someone else could be doing this with Scout.

When an hour had ticked slowly by and enough time had passed after the ponies had been fed, everyone tacked up. Alice fumbled as she tried to do up the buckles on her supple bridle, shaking as she threaded the loose straps through their keepers. Soon after the ponies were led out of their stables, the girls mounted and rode off along Duck Lane.

They turned onto a grassy path alongside a stubble field. After not being able to sleep the night before, Alice was on edge; her jangling, wriggling unease had turned overnight into a leaden feeling in her chest, made up of fear and steely determination. She wasn't going to give Scout up without the biggest fight of her life, but it was a fight she was terrified of losing.

They rode out of one field, across a dirt track then into another field with a grass strip around the barley crop. As soon as Charlie softened her reins Pirate squealed and shot forward, leaping straight into a choppy gallop. Scout bounced, his head up and his ears pricked. Alice squeezed his sides and he plunged forward, bucking excitedly as he chased Pirate. Wish floated behind them, covering the ground effortlessly, her small black Arab hooves barely touching the grass and her creamy mane flowing.

They pulled up as they got to the end of the field, the fit ponies barely blowing as they waited for Dancer to catch up. The strawberry roan cob trundled along at a slow canter, refusing to go any faster. Her big, round hooves thudded the ground as Rosie, pink-cheeked, loudly encouraged her. But Dancer, her ears out sideways and snorting with every stride, wouldn't be hurried.

"Come on, Rosie!" Charlie called urgently. "It would be good to get there today!"

"I'm trying, in case you hadn't noticed!" Rosie puffed crossly as she finally caught up with them. "You try telling Dancer to go fast on a hot summer's day – it's not easy, I can assure you!"

They jogged into the cool shade of the undulating woods. They leaned back in their saddles to help the ponies balance as they headed down the slopes, then cantered up the other sides. They emerged out of the woods and followed the bridleway up the edge of a steep hill, letting their ponies canter on again.

When they got to the top, they stood up in their stirrups and the ponies dropped back to a walk. Below them, at the bottom of the hill, a gate led onto a hedge-lined lane.

"That's it," Mia said, checking her map. "That's Hollow Hill."

Alice stared down at the scattered, uneven row of cottages dotted randomly along the lane. The girls looked across to her and tried to smile. Alice knew that they all felt as nervous as she did. Scout's ears pricked as they rode down the rolling hill and through the gate. Suddenly, Alice started to panic and her mind went blank; she could only remember half sentences of what she'd planned to say to Scarlett. A bolt of fear shot wildly through her, making her heart thunder and her hands start to shake. She took a deep breath. She couldn't afford to get this wrong; it was her best opportunity to keep her favourite pony in the world.

Chapter Five

The handful of cottages were spread out all the way along the lane. Right ahead of them was number one.

"Thirteen must be at the far end," Charlie said, squinting up the lane.

They rode along, Alice's stomach flipping as they trotted past each isolated little cottage, counting them until they got to the last on the right-hand side.

"Um, that's only number twelve," Rosie pointed out, craning her neck to look ahead. "I can't see any more on the other side."

"There must be – we just need to ride further. Come on," Mia said decisively, but as she led the group of four along the lane beside a huge, overgrown bushy hedge on one side, even she started to doubt that there was another cottage tucked away.

They kept walking until they reached a mossy sign, almost hidden by the overgrown hedge that it sat in front of. It read 'Hollow Common'.

"This must be the end of Hollow Hill, then." Mia frowned, halting Wish.

Taking the break as an opportunity to refuel, Dancer lunged towards the tempting hedge and shoved in her nose, taking a big bite. Rosie suddenly got a close-up view of what lay beyond. The hedge was dense, but now she was almost in it, courtesy of Dancer, she could see that it hid a vast, scrubby patch of worn land. The grass looked bare, with patches of vibrant yellow, poisonous ragwort sprouting up everywhere, and beyond the hedge the land was edged with rusty barbed wire. An old tin bath with sharp edges half filled with green, slimy water sat in one corner. There was one old field shelter with a flapping corrugated tin roof over a wooden frame, with holes the size of hooves kicked in it.

"Nothing in there," Rosie announced, struggling to convince Dancer she'd had enough of a fill-up.

"We must have missed it," Charlie said as she spun Pirate round and started to trot back towards where they'd started from.

They rode up the lane past all the cottages and started again at number one. Then, riding slowly and peering everywhere, they headed along the lane once more and stopped by the last cottage, number twelve. It had no curtains at the windows, peeling paint around the frames, and cobwebs across the black, flaking front door and the wonky garden gate. It was the last cottage in the lane, and it was deserted. Beside it they could see a small paddock.

"I don't get it!" Rosie said, counting out the little cottages with her whip in the air. "There is no number thirteen."

Alice looked up and down the lane desperately.

Suddenly a window was thrown open in a cottage further up. A girl, who looked about the same age as them, leaned out.

"Are you lost?" she shouted down, pushing her glasses back up her nose to stop them slipping off.

"No, we're looking for Mrs Valentine and her daughter Scarlett," Mia called back. "She's meant to live in number thirteen..."

"Never heard of her," the girl said, as the others rode their ponies closer to her cottage, "and there's never been a number thirteen on this lane. Mrs Hawk lived in number twelve but she left over a year ago."

The girl at the window was about to dip back inside, but then she suddenly gasped. "Hang on a sec – isn't that Pip?"

She disappeared, leaving the girls looking confused, before reappearing moments later at the front door in a bright green top, denim shorts and trainers. She bobbed over, her wavy blonde hair bouncing with every stride. She made a beeline for Scout.

"It certainly looks like Pip," the girl said warily, stopping a few steps away from the dappled grey. She looked up and saw the girls staring at her. "Oh, sorry. I'm Beth Bright. I *know* this pony – I haven't seen him for a while but I'm *sure* I recognise him."

"Who's Pip?" Rosie asked, making a face. "That pony's called Scout. He was Sunny before that, but never Pip."

"Well, he looks identical," Beth said, sounding uncertain. "Ooh, I know how we could tell for sure – has he got a scar? On his near fore knee?"

The others all looked at Alice, fully expecting her to say no and put an end to the identity mix-up. Instead, Alice went pink and looked flustered.

"*Has* he got a scar there?" Mia asked.

"Well, yes, he has, but..."

"I *told* you it was Pip!" Beth interrupted loudly. "Sammy, who lived next door to us,

used to own him. She kept him turned out in the paddock behind her cottage."

"It can't be the same pony – Mrs Valentine has owned Scout since he was a foal," Alice corrected Beth, certain that she'd made a mistake.

"Anyway, lots of ponies have scars all over the place," Charlie added. "So just because Scout happens to have a scar in the same place it doesn't exactly prove he's Pip."

Beth raised an eyebrow, clearly unconvinced. Mia noticed how sure she looked, though.

"How long did Sammy own Pip for?" she asked, deciding that as Pony Detectives, it was their job to find out as much as they could now they were at Hollow Hill.

"Well, not long as it goes," Beth said, eyeing Scout suspiciously. "One day he totally flipped and threw her on the way back from a ride, pretty much right where you're standing now. No warning, no reason, *nothing*. Sammy's left leg was smashed with a bone poking out and everything!

She had to stay in hospital for ages. Mrs Hawk saw the accident and told us what had happened when we heard all the screaming and came running out to help. By then, Pip had calmed down and was just standing there, shaking. His head was down and there was blood pouring from his knee from where he'd come down on the lane. That's how I know it's him – because of the scar."

"So what happened then?" Charlie asked, intrigued by Beth's story.

"Sammy's parents were so scared of Pip after that that they got rid of him before Sammy even came out of hospital," Beth told them. "I don't blame them either, not after seeing what he did to her."

"So where did this Pip end up?" Rosie asked.

"Well, I don't really know," Beth said. "To begin with Mrs Hawk offered to look after him for Sammy's parents. So he was turned out behind Mrs Hawk's cottage here, for, like, a month or something. Then Mrs Hawk suddenly disappeared.

Overnight. Dad said she was involved in some sort of scandal, something to do with ponies, although I can't remember quite what now. Anyway, Pip disappeared with Mrs Hawk and that was the last I ever heard of him. Till now, that is."

Alice looked down at Scout dozing in the sunshine. None of what Beth said tallied with what Mrs Valentine had told her about Scout's past, and her grey pony would never behave in the way Beth had described. Beth had to be wrong. But then she was *so* convinced, it was difficult to ignore what she said. And Scout did have that scar...

"Did you say Sammy used to live in this lane?" Mia asked. Beth nodded. "I don't suppose you know where she lives now, do you?"

"I can't remember where she moved to. My sister would know, but she's out," Beth said, knitting her brow as she thought and wanting to be helpful. "Ooh – although I do know that she's just taken a nice cob on part loan. He sounds really sweet and reliable from what my sister's said, nothing like *that* crazy pony. Sammy's keeping him at her friend's house – at Hawthorn Farm – she's up there all the time now. Do you know where I mean? Its not far from here."

"That's where Poppy and Moonlight live!" Charlie cried.

"We'll head there now. That way we can double-check Scout's identity by seeing if Sammy recognises him," Mia smiled, relieved that they had something concrete to go on. "Thanks for your help, Beth."

Beth grinned, showing off a brace, then skipped back along the small lane to her cottage's front gate, waving as she ran in through her front door.

"I'm pretty sure Beth's got the wrong pony," Alice said quietly as they set off in the direction of Hawthorn Farm. "I mean, why would Mrs Valentine lie about Scout's past?"

Charlie shrugged. "Beth probably just got muddled up, that's all."

"Although Mrs Valentine did lie about living in Hollow Hill, remember?" Rosie pointed out.

Alice shivered. Rosie had a point, and suddenly her conviction that Beth had got it wrong started to waver.

Chapter Six

The girls rode in silence as they headed off to Hawthorn Farm after quickly checking the map again. They managed to cut across country so that they came to the woods with the natural jumps that they'd found on their way over to Moonlight's yard earlier in the summer.

Alice put all the swirling thoughts to the back of her mind for a moment as she pressed her lower legs to Scout's warm sides. He twitched his ears back to Alice, then bounded forward, cantering eagerly to the row of fences: the log, the stone wall and the tyres. He flew over each one without breaking his stride, his hooves pounding the soft peaty woodland floor. As she patted him, Alice knew that it didn't matter what secrets she found out about Scout's past: nothing would change how much she loved him. But that only made the thought of losing him even harder.

They broke out into the sunshine at the end of the path beyond the woods, patting their ponies, and trotted across the stubble fields until they reached Hawthorn Farm.

They looked into the neat, brick-built stables set back from the drive with their smart green doors and cleanly swept concrete. Hawthorn Farm was where Poppy lived, but her parents rented out the other five stables and they were full of ponies and horses. The only person they knew there was Poppy, so Mia called her name.

Poppy appeared out of a stable, moving a wheelbarrow piled with dirty straw to one side. Her long, naturally straight and sun-bleached hair was pulled back into a floppy ponytail and she looked surprised when she saw the girls waiting for her.

"Hi guys! Everything okay?" she beamed, strolling over to the gate.

Seeing Poppy's bright smile suddenly made Alice wobble as she tried to smile back and explain what they'd come for. Mia noticed Alice struggling and stepped in.

"It's Scout," she explained. "His owner's suddenly turned up and announced that she's selling him. We tried to find her at the address she gave Alice a year ago, in Hollow Hill, only the address doesn't exist and no one's heard of her. But we bumped into someone called Beth, who thought she recognised Scout and said that he used to belong to a girl called Sammy. We're pretty sure that she got it wrong, but we thought we'd better check, just in case."

At that moment a girl with cropped auburn hair, a face full of pale freckles and bright green eyes bobbed out of the tack room.

"Did I hear my name?" she said, looking over to the gate. All of a sudden, the girl's face lit up. "I don't believe it! Pip!"

She ran over with a slight limp and gave Scout

a huge hug. As she stepped back, wiping her eyes, Scout blew hard, then nickered deep in his throat. They clearly recognised each other. Beyond any doubt, Scout *was* Pip, and any hopes that Beth had made a huge mistake vanished in an instant. The shock made Alice go cold and her face felt clammy. Alice looked at Scout; suddenly, it felt as if she was gripping the reins of a pony with a secret past, one that other people knew more about than she did.

"You'd better come in," Poppy said, looking anxiously at Alice, who had turned worryingly pale. "You can put your ponies in one of Dad's spare paddocks and I'll get some drinks."

They led the ponies to the water trough in the yard, where Dancer managed to splurge water over everyone before they untacked. They led them through the gate into the paddock once Poppy had checked that they were all up to date with their worming.

Within minutes the ponies were whizzing

round in the unfamiliar surroundings, rushing up to the fence and arching their necks, and blowing down their noses to Moonlight who was turned out in the field next to them. After squeals and hoof-stomping, they wheeled round again before Wish and Dancer settled and started to graze. Pirate and Scout continued to trot round, their tails and heads high.

Poppy quickly cleared her wheelbarrow away then rushed into the cottage next door. She soon came back out with a tray full of orange juice and home-made fairy cakes.

They decided to go into the light and airy office, with its big desk in one corner piled with bits of paperwork and diaries. Above it hung a huge noticeboard, every inch of it covered with photographs of the various ponies and riders at Hawthorn Farm, along with pictures of the sheep Poppy's dad bred. Along the far wall were a couple of massive, ancient, cat-clawed and ragged but comfy, squishy sofas. The girls all flopped down.

Rosie grabbed two fairy cakes and popped one whole into her mouth before Mia saw her. She tried to smile innocently as Mia watched her suspiciously, only she started to choke, spraying fairy cake crumbs over Mia's immaculate jods. Charlie was about to giggle, until she glanced over and caught the lost look on Alice's face.

When they had all sat down, Mia gave Poppy and Sammy a fuller explanation of the situation while they both sat listening intently. Mia told them how Alice had first fallen in love with Scout as she cycled past Dragonfly Marsh and had taken him on loan after seeing an advert for him in *Pony Mad*. As Mia sipped her drink, Charlie continued telling them how Alice and her parents had met Mrs Valentine at the Marsh and how Mrs Valentine had claimed to have bought Scout for her daughter when he was a foal. Then Scarlett had got ill and could no longer look after him, so Scout had been turned out on the Marsh. Sammy shook her head, knowing they'd been lied to.

"Mrs Valentine never gave Alice the loan agreement she'd promised her at the start," Mia finished. "In fact, Mrs Valentine disappeared completely for a year, and the first time Alice saw her again was yesterday at the show…"

"… when Mrs Valentine turned up out of the blue," Rosie finished, "announcing that Scout was up for sale."

"So you went to Hollow Hill to find Mrs Valentine, but found Beth instead, right?" Sammy asked, looking over at the girls.

Charlie nodded, and explained exactly what Beth had said.

"Well, Beth was partly right," Sammy nodded. "I did own him, and I did fall off and break my leg pretty badly. But it didn't exactly happen the way she told you."

"So how *did* it happen?" Alice asked in a small voice. She was struggling to take everything in, but she had to – she was a Pony Detective after all, and Scout was depending on her. She would have to piece together his past all over again, like a brand new jigsaw puzzle. The information from Beth was the first piece and now, from Sammy, they were about to get the second. She took a jagged breath, picking at a hole in her jods as Sammy started to speak.

"Well, I got Scout when he was just five years old, and my parents weren't that sure about it because they were convinced he was too young," she explained. "But I fell in love with him when I saw his ad in the local paper. I could tell as soon as I tried him that although he was only young he was really sweet natured and sensible. And he never put a hoof wrong until one day when we were coming back from a ride. Just as we walked past number twelve, Mrs Hawk dropped a metal dustbin lid on her garden path. It totally spooked Pip, understandably. His hooves skidded out from under him and he fell over, crushing my leg. But it was weird, because I remember Mrs Hawk watching us riding up the lane.

Then she dropped the lid just as we reached her."

"So it wasn't Scout's fault, then?" Charlie asked, looking over to Alice. Sammy shook her head, frowning.

"Definitely not!" Sammy continued. "Mrs Hawk never owned up to anyone what really happened. I kept trying to tell my parents but they just said that I was covering up for Pip. After the accident she persuaded them to sell Pip, saying that he was dangerous."

"Beth said that Mrs Hawk kept him," Mia pointed out. "Is that right?"

Sammy nodded.

"Apparently, she knew about an auction that was coming up while I was still in hospital, Roger Green Auctions it was, and said that she'd take him and get the highest bid for him," she explained. "But that bid happened to be very low, and from her, so she basically bought him at a knock-down price. I found out afterwards that she kept several horses on Hollow Common, out of sight of the lane. I think she was a dealer of some kind, so I was always worried about what would happen to Pip. Anyway, this all went on when I was in hospital, and when I got out Mrs Hawk had disappeared and Pip had gone too. I never even got to say goodbye."

"So have you ever heard of Mrs Valentine?" Rosie asked, looking puzzled.

Sammy shook her head, looking at Poppy, who said that she hadn't heard of her either.

"But the person you bought Scout – or Pip – off, was she local?" Alice asked.

"She was. It was a lovely woman called Iris Evergreen. She'd had him for a while," Sammy explained, "since he was about three. She broke him in, but I don't know who had him before then, sorry. Iris emigrated to Australia, so couldn't keep him. She was really happy that at least she could see he was going to a good home. I felt like I let her down as well as Pip when he was sold."

"That wasn't your fault, though," Charlie said

as Rosie popped another fairy cake in her mouth.

"What I don't get", Alice said, feeling mystified, "is what happened after Mrs Hawk bought Scout. I mean, where does Mrs Valentine fit in to all this?"

"I guess if Mrs Hawk was a dealer she must have sold Pip on to Mrs Valentine," Poppy suggested.

"Poor Scout," Rosie said through a mouthful of cake. "What bad luck to have two horrible owners in a row."

"Do you remember when Mrs Hawk took Pip to the auction?" Mia asked as she stood up, finding a crumb on her on her pink and purple-starred jods and flicking it off.

"Well, I don't know exactly, but it was when I was in hospital," Sammy said. "So it must have been some time in April last year."

"I took Scout on loan in June," Alice said, stepping back out into the sunshine from the shade of the office and feeling the warmth hit her as she bent down to pick up her tack. "And I saw him for the first time in May, when his frightened little grey face just appeared through the long grass as I cycled along. But if Mrs Hawk bought Scout in April and had him for about a month, Mrs Valentine must only have had him for about two minutes before she put him out onto Dragonfly Marsh."

"So why did she say she'd had him since he was a foal?" Charlie asked, as she and the others called out to their ponies. "Why did she need to lie?"

But as the ponies came thundering over, that was one question none of them could answer.

Chapter Seven

After they'd got back to Blackberry Farm, untacked and turned out the ponies, the girls headed straight round to the hay barn, just beyond the yard. They rushed through the huge open barn doors and bounced over the floor of spilt, loose hay and straw to the round snug of hay bales they'd pulled together. The walls were covered with lots of their favourite pony pics and posters from *Pony Mad*. The air was still; it was cool and peaceful in there, and they could watch the ponies grazing in the paddock.

Mia immediately picked up her notebook and flipped past the page headed 'Moonlight' from their last mystery, and in her neatest writing wrote Scout's name at the top of the new page:

Scout

Alice got a picture of Scout off the barn wall and handed it to Mia, who stuck it in her notebook at the top of the page. Alice shivered seeing his name written there, just like Moonlight's had been at the beginning of the summer when the Pony Detectives had taken on their first case. Now Scout had turned into their second. He might not have been stolen like the piebald, but he was in danger of being taken away from Alice unless they could get to the bottom of the mystery surrounding his past.

As they sat on the edge of the hay bales Mia started to write down all the information they'd picked up that morning while the others pitched in:

1 - Mrs Valentine told Alice that she'd owned Scout since he was a foal and would never, ever sell him because he belonged to her ill daughter, Scarlett.

2 - Mrs V. said Alice could have Scout on permanent loan, but she never sent the loan agreement.

3 - Turns out that Mrs V. didn't own Scout since he was a foal, and that a woman called Iris had him when he was 3, before Sammy bought him when he was 5. He was then sold cheaply at Roger Green Auctions in April last year to Mrs Hawk, who sounds suspiciously like a dealer.

4 - Mrs Valentine must have bought Scout very soon afterwards because Alice discovered him on Dragonfly Marsh in May and took him on loan last June after seeing an advert for him in PONY MAD.

5 - Mrs V. gave Alice a false address - but one

that happened to be right next to where Scout used to be kept, first by Sammy, then by Mrs Hawk.

"There's definitely something seriously dodgy going on," Charlie said, reading the list. "*Nothing* Mrs Valentine's told Alice is true, and we have to find out why before she manages to sell Scout."

Mia chewed her pen thoughtfully.

"Well, one thing's obvious looking at all this: it's pointless us trying to find Scarlett so we can change her mind," she said, "because if she'd only had him for a couple of months, and most of that time he was on Dragonfly Marsh, I seriously doubt she'll be bothered about the prospect of him being sold."

"So that's our first plan of action out of the window," Rosie agreed, dismissing the apples that Mia offered round, and bringing out a slightly squished chocolate bar instead.

"The question is," Mia said quietly, reading

and re-reading the clues and hoping that something would suddenly jump out at her and start making sense, "where do we go from here?"

Chapter Eight

"SORRY I'm here so early." Alice shivered as she sat down at Rosie's kitchen table the next morning, her foot tapping edgily. "I couldn't sleep, so I thought I might as well come over."

"S'fine," Rosie replied. She'd been hauled out of bed almost an hour earlier than usual after hearing Alice's anxious knocking at the door. She sat in her pyjamas and yawned as she cradled a hot chocolate. Mrs Honeycott pottered about in the background, her hair piled up haphazardly on her head, her dressing gown splattered with a rainbow of paint colours. She had been heading for her studio to work on her latest painting when Alice arrived, but before she disappeared she'd put on milk for hot chocolate. She absently patted

Alice on the head, knowing that something was up with her daughter's friend.

Alice drank a few sips of her hot chocolate while Rosie went upstairs to get dressed, but what she really wanted was to be out in the yard, with Scout. She didn't know how long they had left together, and she wanted to spend every second with him that she could. When Rosie reappeared a few moments later in scruffy outgrown navy jodhpurs and a yellow T-shirt, they trooped out of the kitchen, grabbed headcollars and went to collect the four ponies from the paddock. They brought them in, Rosie leading Dancer and Wish, and Alice with Scout and a jogging Pirate. Then they made up the feeds. The ponies ate tied up in the yard outside their stables. As Scout chomped, Alice leaned against his withers trying to take in every detail about him, as if she were recording them in her memory, just in case. She stopped herself, not wanting to believe that Scout might really go.

Then she took a deep breath and went to fetch her grooming kit from the tack room.

When Scout had finished his feed and licked every hidden corner of his bucket, Alice tried to distract herself by grooming him. She fussed around the grey pony, brushing off all the grass stains on his hocks, withers and neck, and making his dapples sparkle. Then she trimmed his feathers, levelled off his tail and pulled his mane to neaten it up. Scout loved nothing more than having tons of attention and he dozed in the early morning sunshine, blinking round at Alice and rummaging in her pockets for treats when she tried to brush his forelock.

She'd just finished when Charlie arrived on her bike. Almost before she'd had a chance to get onto the yard, a car drove up the drive. A door slammed, and a second later Mia came running onto the yard too. Normally Mia was a picture of calm collectedness, whatever the situation, but it was obvious from the moment she stopped in front of Alice, her almond eyes wide, that something had seriously rattled her.

"What's the matter?" Charlie asked, following Mia across the yard. Rosie threw her mane comb back into Dancer's grooming kit and rushed over to join them.

"I glanced behind me in the car as Dad drove here just now," Mia explained, raking her hand through her long, silky black hair. "I don't know what made me look, but there was a car right behind us. When I saw who was driving I made Dad speed up, just so we could get here quicker to give me a chance to warn you!"

The others stared at Mia. At that moment, they heard another car bump down the drive.

"Who was driving?" Rosie asked, looking over to the drive as a sleek dark grey Range Rover appeared near the cottage and parked.

"Mrs Valentine," Mia told them, looking anxiously at Alice.

Alice gasped. Her first panicked thought was

that she should untie Scout, leap on him bareback and gallop him miles into the woods at the back of Blackberry Farm. Her heart started to race as she reached for the lead rope with shaking fingers. But deep down she knew she couldn't hide him among the trees for ever. Or even for a week.

"Did you know she was coming?" Rosie asked, looking dismayed.

Alice frowned, shaking her head and racking her brain over what the unannounced and unexpected visit could possibly be about.

"Maybe she's come to her senses and changed her mind about selling Scout!" Charlie suggested optimistically, squeezing Alice's arm. At Charlie's words, Alice felt a surge of excitement.

"Do you reckon?" she said, almost allowing herself a smile.

"Well, one thing's for sure," Mia said quietly as they heard a car door slam. "At least this gives us a chance to find some answers to the questions we came up with yesterday."

Alice took a huge deep breath to try to steady her nerves as Mrs Valentine appeared on the yard, her sunglasses and large-brimmed hat still in place. She walked straight over to Scout, smiling her approval at his appearance and quietly sizing up the yard. Seeing her smiling face, Alice felt a glow of warmth. Maybe things would be fine after all. Just as she was about to relax the teeniest fraction, she heard a loud rumble from the drive. She looked up and Mrs Valentine followed her gaze, then checked her watch.

"Right on time," she said smoothly.

"Er, what is?" Rosie asked, looking round at the others.

"The first person who's come to try Scout, of course," Mrs Valentine purred.

"What?!" Alice almost choked, feeling her face flush pink and her heart hammer in her throat. "But... but the advert's not due out until the next issue of *Pony Mad*! Scout's not officially for sale yet – no one can come and try him!"

"Well, this is a bit of a *special* trial," Mrs Valentine explained smugly. "You see, I overheard someone asking about me at the Show after I left you. Turned out that this person was particularly keen to buy Sunny – money no object – so obviously I had to introduce myself at once. They persuaded me to let them come and try him today, ahead of the advert coming out. They *so* wanted first refusal. I had meant to call and let you know I'd be coming, but I didn't want you to *forget* and be out, by mistake. I thought it would be better for us just to drop in. So I'm delighted you've got him looking so amazing, without any notice. He looks worth every penny of my asking price, don't you think?"

With that, Mrs Valentine turned on her heel and marched over to the gate.

Alice felt faint. She felt sick. She turned to Scout, who was standing, ears pricked, listening to the engine approaching. She put her arms around his neck and stood there, hardly able to breathe.

"This isn't fair," Rosie whispered hoarsely. "She can't turn up out of the blue like this and just act like Scout's..."

"Hers?" Charlie finished. Rosie huffed. Charlie was right, but it didn't make what she was doing any easier to swallow.

"So who is it that's come to try him?" Mia said, frowning as she tried to work it out, all thoughts of questioning Mrs Valentine dissolving at once. "Who would have been talking about him at the show?"

"There's only one person I can possibly think of..." Charlie said, glancing over at Alice, who had suddenly turned very pale.

At that moment the top of a brightly coloured horsebox became visible above the overgrown hedges lining the track before it swung into the parking area beyond the gate.

More doors slammed, and the next second a girl wearing a bright stripy T-shirt and garish green jodhpurs bobbed round the corner. Before them, grinning like a cat that had got the cream, stood Alice's worst nightmare – Tallulah Starr. Fear gripped Alice as she turned to look at Scout, standing there quietly, trustingly. There was no way that she wanted Tallulah getting her hands on him, just to dump him in a stable to be looked after by someone else, to ruin him then sell him on like a second-hand car for scrap. No way! Not far behind Tallulah was her dad, swaggering and talking in a loud, brash voice to Mrs Valentine, and acting like he owned the yard.

"Hi, Alice." Tallulah smiled brightly, looking straight past Alice to Scout, her eyes loaded with electric blue glittery eyeshadow. "Isn't it funny, you saying at the show that Scout wasn't for sale and now, look – here I am, about to buy him!"

"Here you are," Alice said through gritted teeth.

"Normally, I make my instructors pick out the best ponies for me and I don't bother getting involved – I just ride them when they turn up," Tallulah gushed. "But my last instructor walked out last week, and my groom, too, come to that – I have no idea why – so I had to come and do it myself. Mind you, this is a bit different because I already know that I want Scout, whatever the price. Oh, tack him up, can you, Alice? He's still yours, after all."

As Tallulah continued to chatter away, Alice scowled before disappearing with leaden legs to fetch the tack.

"Still, it's actually really handy that I had to come along today," Tallulah chirped as Alice put the tack on the top of the half stable door. "After all, I intend to win the Sweetbriar Stud Cup on my new pony, so this trial will give him a chance to get used to me. Oh, and I'm changing his name by the way, look! Do you like it?"

Tallulah turned round and pointed to the lettering she'd already had printed on the back of her T-shirt:

Tallulah Starr & Diamond Starr,
sponsored by Starr Cars,
the classiest motors in town

Alice gasped. She felt the blood race through her body and her hands started to shake. She was so angry and frustrated and protective over Scout, and yet so utterly powerless to do anything about Tallulah taking him.

"I think the Sweetbriar Stud Cup's beyond Scout's scope. You could ruin him if you enter it and scare him over a course that's too big," Mia pointed out.

"Don't be ridiculous," Tallulah said dismissively. "I heard Poppy say quite clearly that she thought this pony was a star, and that she'd buy him if she didn't have her piebald. And if *she* likes him, I've got to make sure that I get in there first, before she sees his advert and puts in an offer herself!"

Tallulah decided she should tack Scout up herself after all, 'to help them bond'. He lifted his head sharply as she clonked the bit into his mouth, hitting his teeth, before thumping the saddle onto his back and leading him out of the stable. It was only Charlie grabbing the stable door that stopped it swinging back on him – not that Tallulah even noticed.

She climbed into the saddle and kicked Scout's sides with her heels, asking him to walk on. But she held on tightly to the reins at the same time, confusing him. He nervously took a step back, thinking that was what Tallulah wanted. She gave him a sharp slap down the shoulder with her whip and he shot forward, his ears flat and a startled look on his face. Alice turned away, wanting to call out everything that Tallulah was doing wrong but knowing that she wouldn't listen for a second even if she did.

The four girls watched as Tallulah trotted Scout down to the schooling paddock and got him going on wonky circles, pulling him to a stop, then kicking him forward into trot, pulling him back to halt, then kicking him into canter, and throwing the reins at him.

"He needs lots of transitions to sharpen him up!" Tallulah called out as she flew past in canter with Scout getting faster, his tail held stiffly out behind him and his ears back. Alice could tell that Scout was seriously anxious. After Tallulah had thoroughly confused him with her chopping and changing and frantic aids, she pointed him at the oxer that was left up from the last time the girls had practised their jumping.

Charlie called out to say that she should warm him up over a cross pole first, but Tallulah stuck out her chin and ignored her, kicking Scout into the large square fence. Her other ponies, who were all older schoolmasters, would have ignored Tallulah and set themselves up nicely, but Scout was less experienced. He lengthened his stride, responding honestly to what Tallulah was asking him to do, and met the fence too fast, on too flat and long a stride. He grunted with the effort of stretching over it, trying hard to clear it, but his big jump left Tallulah behind and she sat back in the saddle too soon. Feeling her weight on his back, Scout dipped and his hind legs crashed into the back pole, hitting it so hard that it cracked.

"I knew these fences looked second rate," Tallulah said breathlessly, still beaming as Alice rushed forwards and Scout pulled up on a slightly uneven stride, his ears pointing back. "Not like the shiny new ones I've got at home. He'll go much better over them when I take him back there, I'm sure of it."

"Don't worry, it's just a knock," Mia said to Alice as they reached Scout. Alice nodded, not trusting herself to speak as she bent down next to him. She ran her hand down his leg, but she couldn't see through the blur in her eyes as she thought of Scout's future with Tallulah and her merry-go-round of grooms who were always too busy to give the ponies any fuss. But then ponies weren't there to be loved in Tallulah's book:

they were there to help her fulfil her ambition and get to the top of the showjumping world. That, and to put her ahead of Poppy Brookes.

"I'd better take him over another fence so that he can get used to my technique," Tallulah chimed, filling Alice with horror.

"Oh, no – I think it might be best to leave it there, don't you?" Mrs Valentine stepped in firmly. Having quickly cottoned on to Tallulah's limitations, she clearly didn't want her to fall off over a fence before the deal had been done. "That was only a blip. He's normally so confident."

"He won't be for long if Tallulah keeps riding him into fences like that," Charlie added, quietly enough for Alice not to hear, as they sat back on the paddock fence again.

"Oh, I know he's good, don't worry," Tallulah smirked. "Poppy Brookes said as much. I can't wait to see her face when she sees me riding him at the weekend – she'll be so jealous! I definitely want him, Dad. Let's take him now."

Alice froze. It suddenly clicked – Tallulah and her dad had come in their horsebox! It hadn't registered at first, but now it was suddenly, horribly clear why they'd brought it. Surely they couldn't just leave this second with Scout? Even Tallulah couldn't expect Alice to have a hurried goodbye while she looked on, as if the last year with Scout counted for nothing. She felt her breath come fast and her throat tighten. Her eyes began to sting as she looked towards Tallulah's dad.

"Of course we can take the pony now, princess," he boomed, reaching for his cheque book. "Anything you want. Now, who do I make this payable to?"

"Oh, I'm sorry, Mr Starr," Mrs Valentine said, her smile still in place but failing to keep a hint of irritation out of her voice. "I deal in cash only, no cheques, and I can't let you take him until he's been paid for."

Alice let out a massive sigh, almost laughing

in relief and not even realising that she'd been holding her breath. This bought them more time to stop the sale, to stop her losing Scout. She turned to the others, who were looking as shocked and relieved as she was.

Tallulah huffed, then rode Scout back into the yard and leaped off, throwing the reins at Alice. Scout turned towards Alice, his ears out sideways, and nudged her hard. He leaned his head against her chest for a moment as she hugged him, breathing in his soft, warm, familiar pony smell. As Alice slid the saddle off his back and the bridle over his ears, gently letting the bit come out of his mouth, she could hear Tallulah, her dad and Mrs Valentine talking. Moments later, Tallulah pranced back to Scout's stable.

"Dad's just arranged everything," she smiled. "He's going away later this morning on a business trip. He doesn't get back till Friday lunchtime, but Mrs Valentine's agreed to cancel the advert and keep the pony just for me. So, Dad's arranged to meet her back here at three o'clock on Friday. Then he'll be all mine and I can take him home there and then. Only that doesn't leave me much time to prepare him for the Sweetbriar Stud show, so you'll have to give him a shampoo for me ready for when I pick him up – okay?"

Tallulah smiled sweetly, while Alice fumed quietly inside. She wasn't Tallulah's new groom, even though Tallulah was acting as if she was.

With that, she said that she'd 'pop in' the day before collecting the pony to measure him up for rugs. She leaned over his stable door and gave him a quick hard pat that sent him scuttling sideways. He let out a long, juddering sigh before turning to his haynet and taking a pull at it distractedly. Tallulah skipped out of the yard, chattering incessantly as the horsebox started up and drowned out her voice.

They heard another engine purr into life.

"I almost forgot," Mia said urgently, running towards the gate, "we still need to get some answers out of Mrs Valentine! Quick, before she drives off!"

They all rushed round to the drive. The horsebox was slowly manoeuvring into it, briefly blocking Mrs Valentine in. It was a hot day, and Mrs Valentine had her windows open. Her handbag was lying on the passenger seat, her mobile phone beside it. Mrs Valentine looked up and smiled.

"I told you the first person to see that pony would buy him," she said with a touch of triumph in her soft voice. "And I was right, wasn't I? Now, I really must go."

"Oh, before you do," Mia said quickly, "we've just got a few questions."

Mrs Valentine glanced up the drive. The horsebox was still manoeuvring so she was still stuck.

"I really don't have time," she said casually. "Maybe another day?"

"Well, this won't take long," Mia replied, "and

you can't exactly go anywhere right now, anyway."

A flash of irritation crossed Mrs Valentine's face. She waved her hand, and Mia took this as a signal for her to carry on.

"We went to your address yesterday," she said, "the one you gave Alice when she took Scout on loan last year."

"And?" Mrs Valentine replied, her stare fixed on the horsebox ahead.

"It doesn't exist," Charlie said.

"Alice must have written it down wrong," Mrs Valentine said coolly, revving her engine.

"And we found out that you'd lied about Scarlett owning Scout since he was a foal," Mia continued, determined not to be put off.

Mrs Valentine glanced up the drive. The horsebox was slowly moving off, but not fast enough. Suddenly, she turned to look at the girls. For the first time, her face was steely. Even from behind her glasses her glare was distinctly icy. Alice wondered how she'd never seen this mean side before as Mrs Valentine's voice became a hiss.

"Now, you listen here! Sunny is *my* pony, and he is up for sale. Nothing you might ask or find out is going to change the situation – got that? So don't go poking your noses in where they don't belong – that's a warning."

The mobile phone on Mrs Valentine's passenger seat startled them all as it burst into life. Charlie just glimpsed the flashing screen. All she saw was one letter – 'R' – before Mrs Valentine snatched it and pressed it to her ear.

"Another one?" she said cryptically. "Good. I'll see you this Thursday, in that case."

Mrs Valentine ended the call. The horsebox was turning out of the drive. Mrs Valentine revved the engine, then in a shower of gravel she shot forward, a smile spreading across her face.

Chapter Nine

"TALLULAH! Of all the people in the world!" Alice sighed for the five hundredth time the next morning as they stood about in the yard while their ponies ate their breakfast. Alice scuffed a weed with her foot, imagining all kinds of horrible scenarios – the worst being that after a few months of Tallulah ruining him, Scout would be up for sale again and would end up being passed from one person to the next, getting more and more scared, more and more lonely, with no one to love him.

"But at least there's a silver lining to this admittedly very big black cloud," Charlie said, trying to sound hopeful as Alice wiped away another tear.

"Er, like the biggest thunder cloud you could ever imagine!" Rosie added helpfully, picking up Pumpkin, the ginger yard cat. He rubbed his head against her chin, purring loudly.

"But the silver lining is that at least we've got until three o'clock on Friday, when Tallulah's dad is coming with the money," Charlie continued, nudging Rosie. "That gives us a bit of time to work out why Mrs Valentine warned us off. It's obvious there's something she doesn't want us to discover. If we can find out what it is we might be able to stop this sale."

"Well, we know from the phone call that she's got something on this Thursday," Mia added, looking hopeful. "If we can find out what that is, and who 'R' is, that might give us another lead."

"We could trail her! See where she goes!" Rosie piped up, excited.

"Considering we don't even know where she lives," Charlie said, "that might be a bit tricky."

At that moment their thoughts were interrupted

as they heard a van rattle and bump down the track and a car horn bip-bip.

Beanie raced to the gate, followed by the girls, as Jock Beamish, their farrier, climbed out of his Land Rover, waving to them as he went round to the back to get out his gear. His own dog, a black labrador called Henry, leaped down and went flying around the yard with Beanie, barking and rolling about excitedly.

Jock, who earned the nickname from his time as a National Hunt jockey before he retrained to be a farrier, lugged his gear into the yard. He stood and wiped his old, furrowed brow for a moment then dragged his hand across his heavy leather chaps, smiling all the while.

The girls loved it when he turned up at Blackberry Farm, as regular as clockwork and always on time, every six weeks, to shoe the ponies. They rushed about, making him tea which they slopped over the edges of the cup onto the yard in their hurry to rush back, and offering him biscuits, slices of home-made fruit cake and thick wedges of bread spread thickly with butter and jam.

The girls would all crowd round as he spoke slowly, his low gentle voice lulling the ponies to sleep. He told them about stealing the Gold Cup in the dying strides on a huge, raw-boned bay, Faraway Kingdom, and storming the Grand National by ten lengths on the small but bold grey, Dreamer's Town. In between raising clenches on the nails, easing off shoes, knocking new ones into shape and taking the long, dark nails one by one from his mouth to tap in, he would regale them with stories from his racing days. He told them the secrets of the weighing room and all the practical jokes the jockeys used to play on each other, and the best way to ride a fence at speed. Rosie always made him repeat that bit, stating that she needed to know for when she jumped Dancer, making the others giggle as they all knew Dancer was the slowest jumper in the universe.

As Mia, then Charlie and Rosie led their ponies out one by one, Jock worked away between slurps of hot, sweet tea and mouthfuls of Victoria sponge cake, whistling almost under his breath to the ponies whenever he wasn't talking. When they were finished, Alice led out Scout.

Jock stood looking at his neat black hooves for a moment before moving with a slight arthritic limp ("from too many years riding in the rain") to stand behind Scout.

"Any problems?" Jock asked Alice slowly.

Alice sighed and shook her head. "Not with his hooves, anyway."

Jock bent and picked up Scout's near fore, expertly taking the shoe off in no time before carefully scraping his sole, talking away quietly as much to soothe Scout as to make conversation.

"I remember the state this boy's hooves were in when I first saw them after he'd been living on Dragonfly Marsh," Jock said, gently shaking his head. "But you're not alone, are you, boy? I've shod a few of you that have come off there in the last year, all with the same hooves. Soft they are, from standing day and night in that wet marshland. It don't take long for a hoof to turn if it's not being checked each day, that's for sure."

The girls had been closing their eyes like Scout and enjoying the sun while they sat on upturned buckets and listened to Jock. In an instant, they jumped up and looked at each other, nearly tipping over their makeshift seats, and startling Scout.

"Hang on," Mia said, swishing her black hair over her shoulder, suddenly alert. "Are you saying other ponies have been grazed on Dragonfly Marsh, besides Scout, I mean?"

"I am indeed saying that," Jock replied, wiping his brow with a look of surprise as he saw the four girls' faces all staring at him intently. "Important, is it?"

"Could be." Alice nodded, suddenly getting excited. "I know Mrs Valentine said she only had Scout, but nothing else she's told me so far is true.

So, I wonder if she owned any other ponies on there, too...?"

Jock frowned, and Mia, Charlie and Rosie rapidly brought him up to speed.

He listened quietly, tilting his head, then smiled kindly, draining his cup in one big swig.

"Well, let me see if I can help you four," Jock mused. He paused for a moment, then continued. "The first time I noticed this kind of hoof was on young Scout here, and since then I've seen a few of them, one here, then one there, spread out all round this county. I always check where they come from, though – hard to miss it. Hooves from the Marsh are like a fingerprint, identifying any pony that's been kept on it as clear as day. It doesn't matter if they're shod or not, it's the insides, the frog and the sole that turn soft standing in all that wet land."

"So how many ponies with hooves like this do you think you've seen?" Charlie asked, getting excited.

Jock smoothed Scout's hoof with a rough hand. "In total, including Scout? About six, I'd say. Now I come to think on it, it's been pretty regular – one every two months or so, I'd reckon."

Mia ran to get her notebook as Jock pulled a small, worn diary out of his back pocket. He flicked through the pages, then began to write a list of the names of the owners, their phone numbers and a description of the ponies that he'd shod that had been on Dragonfly Marsh. The girls looked at each other, convinced that Jock's new information had to be significant.

"We need to speak to the owners to find out who they got their ponies from," Mia said, her mind starting to whir as she realised what this new information might mean for their case.

"And you're sure that these ponies are all ones that have come from the Marsh?" Rosie asked, frowning. The others looked at her reproachfully. Jock never mistook a hoof.

He nodded at Rosie with a wry smile, then

went back to rasping Scout's hooves, making sure that every clench was smoothed over so that they couldn't catch on anything.

"Right, we need to start calling these numbers," Charlie said, pulling out her phone.

"And try to work out who 'R' is, and what's happening tomorrow," Mia agreed, reading back over the clues in the notebook and seeing the one that they'd added after Mrs Valentine's phone call at the yard the day before.

Jock leaned over the notebook, frowning as he started to gather up his tools.

"'R'? Tomorrow?" he said, pausing for a moment with his rasp and hammer in his hand. "I'm on official farrier duty tomorrow morning, at a Roger Green auction. I wonder if that's anything to do with it?"

Alice squealed, suddenly brightening and clapping her hands. "That has to be it! It can't just be a coincidence – Mrs Hawk bought Scout from a Roger Green auction, and Mrs Valentine must have bought him from Mrs Hawk."

"I bet it's all connected!" Mia said excitedly.

"Any chance you've got room to take the four of us?" Rosie asked hopefully. "We can help hold your hammer and nails…?"

Jock smiled. "If it helps young Alice here keep Scout, and your parents say you can come, I'll happily have you as my guests."

Chapter Ten

"Is anyone else wondering how many daughters Mrs Valentine has actually got?" Rosie asked as Mia ended another phone call from the numbers on Jock's list.

They were sitting out in the field with the ponies grazing around them, coming up to them occasionally to nibble the girls' outstretched boots. They were all enjoying their day off in the field after being turned out once Jock left the yard.

"Well, she's either got lots of daughters..." Mia agreed, putting a tick against another name on Jock's list.

"... who all just happen to be ill," Charlie pointed out.

"… or one ill daughter with lots of ponies that she supposedly can't bear to part with," Rosie finished.

"And all the ponies just happen to be called Sunny," Alice added quietly, standing up and scratching Scout's withers until his top lip jutted out and he turned his head to nibble Alice's back. "I guess that makes it easier for Mrs Valentine to remember…"

As they'd sat with the ponies after Jock left, Mia had called all the numbers he'd written down to ask the people on the list about their ponies. All five people on the list had agreed to talk, especially when Mia introduced herself. Mia and Wish had won in the showing ring all around the county, so even though the phone numbers were spread right out they'd all heard of her.

It turned out that all the people on the list had responded to adverts placed in *Pony Mad.* All the ponies had started off on permanent loan. Three ponies were still on what the owners took to be permanent loan, although none of them had been given loan agreements. And none of them had heard from Mrs Valentine since taking on the ponies. They all said how much they'd put into the ponies, who meant even more to them after coming off the Marsh looking a bit bedraggled and scared. Mia glanced at the others as one of the owners said how well their 'Sunny' was starting to do at shows, and how lucky they were to have an owner like Mrs Valentine because she never interfered. Mia thanked them, then called the next number on the list.

The fourth owner told Mia she'd taken Sunny on loan just a couple of months after Alice had got Scout. This pony had already been sold. The story sounded amazingly similar to Scout's: Mr Hackett's daughter, Rebekah, had seen an advert and they'd met Mrs Valentine by Dragonfly Marsh. The pony had looked promising, but it was definitely in need of care and attention and lots of schooling. After they took 'Sunny' on loan, Mrs Valentine had disappeared. Rebekah had clicked instantly with the pony and after lots of schooling they started to take dressage competitions by storm. Then Mrs Valentine had reappeared suddenly, announcing that 'Sunny' was for sale. When Mr Hackett had said that he couldn't afford the huge price she was asking, Mrs Valentine had changed from charming to snakelike in an instant. The pony was sold, leaving Rebekah devastated.

The last number on the list provided a similar story. This time Mrs Wright took their 'Sunny' on loan for her son, Josh. It was his ambition to become a jockey and he patiently trained his pony until he began to win on the pony racing circuit. Mrs Wright had been infuriated when Mrs Valentine appeared and told them she was putting 'Sunny' up for sale for a hugely inflated price.

"She didn't care that me and Josh had put all the money and effort in to turn him into a winner," Mrs Wright explained with a sigh, "so we ended up getting a bank loan to afford to keep him."

As Mia ended the final phone call, scribbling down more information in her notebook, it confirmed their suspicions that nothing Mrs Valentine had told Alice about Scout was true, or was special to him. Mrs Valentine had no idea about the history of the pony she was selling. More to the point, she didn't seem to care.

"One thing," Mia said, carefully studying the rough dates she'd been given for the ponies being advertised and taken on loan. "It looks from these dates that each time one pony was taken on loan, another turned up on Dragonfly Marsh to replace it. Every two months, just like Jock said."

"How mean's that?" Rosie said, plucking at the grass beside her crossly. "Imagine being turned out on that huge, scary marsh without any company. Mrs Valentine really must be hard-hearted, that much is clear. I feel sorry for Scarlett, having a mum like that."

"If Scarlett even exists," Alice said as she flumped back down on the grass after giving Scout some more fuss. "I mean, I never met her. I just heard about her from Mrs Valentine."

"I reckon it *must* be a scam!" Mia concluded. "Mrs Valentine gets hold of cheap ponies and turns them out on Dragonfly Marsh. She doesn't bother taking care of them, but advertises them for loan and gives the unsuspecting person who turns up to try them a sob story about why she can't possibly sell them. They all think they've got the ponies for life and put everything into them!"

"That way she gets someone else to take them on, feed them up and school them," Charlie continued, "then when they've improved hugely she steps in out of nowhere and announces that they're for sale!"

"Making Mrs Valentine a fat profit in the process, without having had to do any of the work *or* spend any money herself," Rosie said indignantly.

"And leaving lots of people broken-hearted," Alice sighed, wishing that Scout hadn't done so well over the summer holidays at all the shows. She was convinced now that Mrs Valentine had been keeping an eye on her from a distance, waiting for signs of serious improvement before swooping.

"And no prizes for guessing where she finds her cheap ponies," Mia said, stroking Wish's soft muzzle as she cropped the grass beside her.

"Roger Green Auctions," Rosie, Alice and Charlie all piped up in unison. Wish stopped grazing for a second, her big brown eyes peeping through her long cream forelock, as she swished away a fly with her tail.

"Well, if it is," Mia said, "we won't have too long to wait before finding out."

"Talking of that, what are we going to wear tomorrow?" Charlie asked, looking round at the others. "If we turn up like this, Mrs Valentine will recognise us in a second..."

"We need disguises!" Rosie exclaimed, holding her finger in the air. "And I know where we might be able to find some!"

Rosie raced into the cottage with the others following her, giggling as they thundered up the stairs. At the top Rosie stood on tiptoe and pushed a hatch door, then she pulled down a ladder and led them up into a dusty, stuffy attic. Rosie tugged a light pull and a bare bulb flashed on, swinging brightly in the eaves.

"Mum's got some old bits and pieces in here that we might be able to use..." Rosie said, flinging open some dust-laden cardboard boxes and rummaging around in them. "There's still loads of stuff we haven't unpacked since we moved..."

Mia glanced around at the dust and chaos surrounding them with a look of mild horror, then carefully prised open the nearest box. She picked through the contents with the tips of her fingers, while next to her Rosie was busy throwing the insides of another box over her shoulder in her search.

"Nice!" Charlie laughed, opening a shoebox and finding an old picture of Rosie sitting on a swing with some seriously dodgy clothes on and an even dodgier haircut, before turning her attention to a different pile.

Alice started to unwrap the newspaper around a tray of face paint.

"Ooh!" Rosie suddenly squealed, leaning over Alice's shoulder. "Look!"

"Okay, stop right there!" Mia exclaimed, noticing at once where Rosie was looking. "There is no way I'm putting that greasy make-up on as a disguise, not for anything. Sorry, Alice."

"I'm not talking about the make-up!" Rosie tutted, picking up the bit of paper that Alice had just dropped. "I was talking about this!"

As Mia leaned in to get a closer look, Rosie started to sneeze wildly. Mia squealed as she got sprayed, setting off Charlie and Alice.

"Rosie, we're meant to be looking for disguises," Charlie said when she'd recovered, "not reading bits of old newspaper."

"But this might be important," Rosie said as she scanned down the page. "Listen: 'Woman Flees Following Pony-Owning Ban'! You'll never guess who it is!"

"Mrs Valentine?" Alice said hopefully, trying to see what Rosie was reading.

"Guess again," Rosie said, looking round at each of them like a quizmaster.

"Just get on with it, Rosie!" Charlie said, striking gold as she pulled out a bright red wavy wig. She shoved it on, getting some dust up her nose and starting to sneeze too, sending the wig falling over her face.

"Okay, okay," Rosie replied, "keep your hair on."

"Never mind all that," Mia said impatiently. "Who's it about?"

"Mrs Hawk," Rosie announced dramatically,

her face lit up unnaturally as she knelt below the light bulb.

The others all looked over at the crumpled page from Rosie's old local paper while she read it out:

> A LOCAL WOMAN has gone on the run after a number of ponies owned by her were found on Hollow Common, near Hollow Hill, in poor condition. The field they were grazing could not be seen from the roadside.
>
> All the ponies have been seized by the RSPCA after the identity of the local woman was revealed as that of Mrs Nora Hawk (47). She already faced a ban from owning ponies after neglecting them in the past. It's now understood that Mrs Hawk has previously been on the run, in an attempt to avoid detection

– and the ban. However, once she moved into this county she flouted the ban and continued to buy and sell ponies.

Local residents were shocked by the news.

"Mrs Hawk always kept herself to herself and I had no idea this was happening just down the road from me," said one Hollow Hill resident, Mr Colin Bright (38). "I didn't know anything about the ponies on Hollow Common because it's hidden, but I do know she had a pony in the paddock out the back of her cottage when she disappeared."

Mrs Hawk left her Hollow Hill address in the middle of the night with this particular pony and fled once more before the ban could be issued. Any news on her whereabouts should be reported to

> the RSPCA immediately. She is described as tall and thin, with short black hair. She is considered extremely devious.

At the end of the article was a grainy black-and-white photo of a woman with short dark hair and small, beady eyes.

"Mr Bright – that must be Beth's dad," Charlie said after they'd looked at the picture. "Beth *said* that Mrs Hawk had been involved in some kind of scandal when she left."

"The date on this newspaper's April the twenty-ninth," Mia pointed out.

"Sammy said Mrs Hawk bought Scout at auction in April," Alice said, frowning. "If the RSPCA had seized all her other ponies from Hollow Common and were onto her, she'd have had to sell Scout in a serious hurry. Mrs Valentine must have picked him up really cheaply, I bet."

"And now she's trying to sell him on for a huge profit," Rosie tutted.

"This doesn't just mean there's a link between Mrs Valentine and all the ponies on Dragonfly Marsh," Mia said. "It confirms what we'd all suspected – that there's also a link between Mrs Valentine and not just any old dealer, but a very dodgy one in Mrs Hawk."

As the four girls sat among the boxes and discarded paper they suddenly realised that the case had taken a sinister twist. They sat stony-faced, until Rosie glanced sideways and suddenly perked up.

"Bingo!" she cried, pulling some old baseball caps out of a box. "Our disguises!"

Chapter Eleven

Jock hooted outside Blackberry Farm's gate at seven thirty the next morning, ready for the hour's drive ahead. The girls had all slept over at the farm ready for their early start, and they'd already been out in the yard, mixing feeds and taking them out for their ponies to eat in the field. After they'd got back in, Rosie, Alice and Charlie had groaned as they lounged across the kitchen table yawning, their dusty baseball caps pulled low over their faces. Mia, who was refusing to wear hers until the very last possible moment, had piled her glossy black hair up first thing in preparation while Mrs Honeycott made everyone tea and thick slices of toast with melted butter and strawberry jam.

“Mia, it’s officially wrong that you can look so neat and together this early in the morning,” Rosie sighed as she heard the toot and scraped back her chair. She called out goodbye to her parents, and kissed Beanie, who was rustling round the kitchen, and Pumpkin, who was curled up near the Aga.

“I don’t know how you do it,” Charlie agreed sleepily as she pushed her brown fringe under the peak of her hat.

“It’s a talent, I know.” Mia smiled sweetly as they bundled out of the cottage and clambered into Jock’s jeep, clanging shut the rattly door and saying hello.

As Jock drove, the girls chattered away, laughing as they got bounced around on the hard seats every time they went over the tiniest bump in the road. They told him what they’d uncovered about Mrs Hawk, which he remembered hearing about at the time, and described Mrs Valentine to him. He agreed to keep an eye out for her too.

Rosie somehow managed to doze as they rattled along until Charlie, realising they were getting close, gave her a nudge. She'd caught sight of the brush fences and white rails curling around the smooth green turf of their local point-to-point racetrack where the auction was being held. As they craned their necks, they saw a huge, slightly grubby-looking marquee with 'Roger Green Auctions' emblazoned in a rich emerald green across the arch of a tunnel, which led to a circular main tent.

Jock wound down his window as they turned off the busy road and bumped across an uneven field. He announced himself as the official farrier, making the girls feel very important, before being waved off to park on the right. He rumbled forward, then ground to a juddering halt in the area of the car park reserved for 'officials', away from a huge mass of ancient trailers and old horseboxes. As the humming engine was switched off, its noise was replaced at once by the buzz of hundreds of voices.

As soon as they jumped out into an already sweltering day, Alice, Charlie, Mia and Rosie were almost swallowed up by the people bustling backwards and forwards. It was still early but the air was filled with the smell of burgers, horse manure and lots of people packed in together. They made their way through the crowds from the car park, past ponies which were already being exercised in far corners of the field, with numbered stickers on their rumps. They continued past the temporary stables where they could hear the shrill neighs of hundreds of nervous horses and ponies. They were being led in and out and trotted up on the wide concrete walkways in front of groups of potential buyers.

"I had no idea it would be so busy!" Rosie squealed, narrowly missing being trotted over by a huge grey horse as they made their way to the auction tent.

Mia peered down the roped entrance into the gloom beyond and saw a ring with sawdust in the middle and rows of metal-framed seats curled around it. On the opposite side was the auctioneer's rostrum, a wooden, boxed-in platform about waist height with a wide shelf. Mia saw a vast man with a yellow checked waistcoat and a large, ruddy face leaning forward over it. He watched everyone who wandered in closely over his half-moon glasses, his eyes darting in every direction as he rubbed a bushy moustache. A few people called out and he waved to them, replying in a deeply booming rich voice.

They paused for a moment outside the tent as the next 'lot', a tall, temperamental-looking bay, disappeared down into the tunnel out of sight. They heard the auctioneer's quick-fire sales chatter start at once and pick up into a continuous crescendo, floating out of the ring to where they were standing.

"He can't have time to breathe!" Charlie laughed as they listened to his voice rising and falling, getting the bidding started and then taking the price up without a pause. He could be heard encouraging everyone inside the tent to have a go, listing all the pony's good points in any of the gaps between bids before racing up through the increases. Suddenly, the bidding stopped. The girls listened, peering down into the ring, and caught sight of the auctioneer going round the ring encouraging more buyers to join in, announcing that lot 23 was going once, twice, then a dramatic pause before the final slamming hammer fall.

"Sold!"

Alice stood back from the roped entrance as the bay horse, which had started to sweat up, jogged out of the marquee. He was followed by an excited-looking couple who walked with the handler back to the stables. The girls watched as the next lot, a small chestnut pony, trotted towards the ring, the whites of his eyes showing. There was a scuffle of hooves as he refused to enter for a moment, half rearing and pulling back on the reins. Alice could see his sides heaving as he neighed at the top of his voice, trying to turn his head back to the stable block before finally barging forward into the ring.

She wondered if Scout had been as terrified with all the commotion and strange sounds and smells bombarding him when he'd been brought to the sale. She wished for a second that she could rush up and hug the pony, tell him he would be all right, but she couldn't. He had disappeared and the bidding was starting, the auctioneer racing off at high speed until the hammer fell and the pony was led out. Alice felt relieved as she saw a young boy and his parents rush to meet the pony, thinking that at least it looked as if he'd gone to someone who'd love him as much as she loved Scout.

"Right, we need to focus," Mia announced after they'd each bought ice-cold cans of fizzy drink from a nearby stand. "The auction is only on this morning, so we don't have long."

"And what exactly is it we're meant to be focusing on again?" Rosie asked as she snapped back the ring pull on her can and took a glug of drink. It was so cold that the bubbles went up her nose and made her eyes water.

"Mrs Valentine," Charlie said, squinting into the sun, "and I think I might have just found her..."

The others followed Charlie's gaze and saw a tall, wiry woman dressed smartly all in navy, with a floppy hat, long blonde hair and huge dark sunglasses, slip across from the car park and disappear in front of them through the crowds and into the marquee.

"Quick – don't lose sight of her!" Mia instructed as they ducked down and raced forward, bumping into each other. They rushed into the relative gloom of the marquee. Keeping low, they tiptoed up the metallic stairs then dived into some seats halfway up, sitting right by the entrance where there were thick metal frames to the edges of the seats to give them some cover.

Alice pulled her baseball cap down and noticed the others do the same while they furtively looked around.

"There she is!" Alice whispered, nudging Rosie, who had spotted her too. She was sitting in the middle, further along on the same side as them but right at the bottom of the rows of seats. Their position was perfect. The girls could see her, but she had no idea they were there.

"I wonder what she's up to," Rosie said quietly as Mrs Valentine nodded discreetly at the auctioneer. He ever so slightly raised his gavel towards her, acknowledging her arrival, before turning his attention back to a spotted pony in the ring.

"That's what we're about to find out... " Mia replied, as she held one hand up to her cap.

Charlie and Alice exchanged glances, jiggling their legs with nervous excitement, hoping that at any second Mrs Valentine was going to do something obviously underhand. They just didn't have a clue what it might be.

A couple of hours later, after what seemed like a thousand lots had walked and trotted in and out of the ring, they were still sitting there, feeling slightly less excited, their legs stiff and their eyes glued to Mrs Valentine's slightest move. Rosie shifted in her seat, aching from the hard metal.

"Do you think she's actually going to do *any*thing?" Charlie asked, checking her watch. At this rate Jock was going to be collecting them before Mrs Valentine had even got going.

"Maybe she's just come to buy a pony, and there's nothing dodgy going on after all," Rosie suggested, her stomach starting to rumble as another horse walked out of the ring, this time without being sold.

"But if she was buying she'd have a catalogue, wouldn't she? Just like everyone else who's been bidding," Charlie pointed out, wondering if they were on a wild goose chase.

They looked over to the entrance, but no other horse came in and the auctioneer announced that it was time for a short break. Rosie checked her watch. It was getting near to twelve o'clock. Almost lunch time. Her face brightened instantly.

"Perfect, I'm just going to nip out to grab a burger..."

Just as Rosie went to stand up Mia suddenly pulled her back down and the four of them almost fell off their seats, ducking behind the ones in front. Mrs Valentine was finally on the move. They waited until she'd walked through the tunnel before clattering over the seats, jumping down the last few steps and rushing after her. They kept their heads low, their eyes fixed on the wide-brimmed hat that bobbed through the crowds.

"She's heading for the stables!" Alice whispered as they hopped between the groups of chattering people. They kept their distance, with their eyes glued to the hat as it disappeared into the temporary stable block nearest to the auction ring.

The block was open at both ends, with horses and ponies in stables facing each other. Mrs Valentine glided straight through the wide walkway in the middle, not stopping to check any ponies as everyone else around her was doing, or even to pat one of the noses poking out. It was noisy in there, the air filled with people chatting and laughing, and with ponies neighing and metallic clangs as hooves kicked out against the dividers. It was only when Mrs Valentine got to the far end of the stable block that she hesitated for a moment.

The girls instinctively turned to pat the nearest pony, pulling down their baseball caps and bunching up together. Rosie glanced over and noticed that Mrs Valentine was standing by the last stable, checking over the stable door, before having a furtive look around. Rosie quickly glanced down at the floor. When she turned back, Mrs Valentine was gone.

They hurried to the far end of the stables, poking their heads carefully around the edge. A few metres beyond the last stable, outside the block, they saw the auctioneer step out of a tent flap at the rear of the marquee. They quickly ducked back round the edge of the stables.

"That flap must be just behind his rostrum," Mia whispered under her breath.

They heard a delicate cough, and with a flutter of their hearts they realised that Mrs Valentine was lurking just outside the end stable. Mia nervously looked around her. They needed to hide: if Mrs Valentine and the auctioneer walked back into the stables, they'd see them at once.

"In here." Mia pointed, quietly drawing back the bolt on the last stable. They all piled in with a docile-looking chestnut horse who stood resting one back leg, her eyes sleepy. They crowded round the small, open window that looked out onto the area where Mrs Valentine was standing. They could just about make out the conversation. Mia pulled her phone from her pocket and started taking a video, holding the camera slightly above the open window so that she could pick up the voices.

"So how are our 'investments' going?" the man asked, hushing his deep, huge voice.

"Very well, Roger. I've got another one *maturing* tomorrow," Mrs Valentine replied, a thin smile in her voice. "So you'll get your slice very soon. It's a good one, too."

"That's what I like to hear." Roger laughed greedily and mopped his hairy brow. "I've got another one for you too, lot 107 – next one in the ring. Nicely put together chap, fallen on hard times but should make someone a super all-rounder. The plan's the same as usual: I'll keep the price low for you, in return for my share of the profits when you sell."

"Of course, Roger. After all, why change

a winning formula?" Mrs Valentine smirked. "Lot 107, here we come."

Roger Green nodded, with a wide, satisfied grin, as Mrs Valentine turned on her heel and reappeared in the stables. Rosie, Alice, Charlie and Mia all bent over at once, suddenly paying a lot of attention to the chestnut's hooves.

"Are you interested in her?" A voice called out. They turned to see a friendly-looking man standing by the door.

"Oh, er, no, just checking her hooves, that's all," Rosie explained, trying to make herself look official, tapping her nose and making the others giggle. "We're with Jock, the farrier, you see."

"Oh, right," the man replied, looking confused, as the girls raced down the stable block and re-took their seats just as lot 107 entered the ring and the auction re-started.

Immediately, the difference in Roger Green was obvious. He remained quiet, as a sweet dun pony, who looked a bit uncared for, walked in nervously. Roger spooked him each time he was paraded past him, by dropping his hammer or coughing suddenly, and the little pony grew increasingly jittery. Normally, Roger would be into his sales chatter by now but this time he remained silent for some time before gradually building up. The enthusiasm in his voice was missing; he wasn't drumming up any interest. There was only one bidder: Mrs Valentine. She waited for as long as possible before raising her hand. Another person entered the bidding for a couple of minutes, and there were a few rises in price, but with Roger's subdued commentary the dun was quickly knocked down cheaply to Mrs Valentine. She hurried from the ring with a secretive smile as the girls hid their faces.

"So *that's* what she's up to!" Mia shook her head as they jumped down the stairs and followed the hat once more. "Roger Green keeps the price low for certain ponies who have potential but who are looking a bit ragged, and Mrs Valentine buys them, puts them out on loan then sells them once they've been improved."

"Then she splits the profits with Roger!" Charlie added as they saw Mrs Valentine disappear into a small Portakabin which had a printed sign saying 'SALES' on the door.

"And the one 'maturing' tomorrow", Alice said, her stomach lurching at the thought, "must be Scout."

They stood just outside the Portakabin, straining to hear as Mrs Valentine filled in the necessary paperwork, getting the dun pony signed over to her. They heard her counting out money. She wasted no time on small talk, and they soon heard her step out of the office and saw her head off in the direction of the stables. Keeping their caps pulled down, they watched as she quickly reappeared leading the dun pony and headed towards the car park with its hundreds of horseboxes.

They tried to keep behind Mrs Valentine but

got blocked by the crowds. Just as they started to get closer at the edge of the car park, a stern-faced attendant in a hi-viz jacket stepped in front of them.

"You girls can't go into that horsebox park unaccompanied," he announced solemnly. "Sorry."

The girls watched Mrs Valentine frantically as the dun pony was swallowed up among the sea of horseboxes.

"Quick, we've got to find Jock!" Charlie cried.

"Ah, I was just looking for you four."

The girls turned. They'd never been so glad to see anyone.

"Perfect, because we have to go, like now!" Rosie said urgently, pulling on his arm. "Mrs Valentine's bought a new pony. She's taken him over to the car park so she must be about to load him in her trailer before making her escape!"

"We know what she's up to," Alice explained as quickly as she could when she saw Jock frowning, "but we didn't get a chance to confront her before she disappeared into the horsebox park. The only chance we've got now to challenge her about what she's doing is if we follow her trailer – then we'll find out where she lives and we can talk to her there instead!"

"If we don't," Mia added, "the next chance we'll get won't be until tomorrow, when she comes to collect the money from Tallulah's dad and it'll be too late by then – Scout will be sold! We have to talk to her today, now we know what her game is – it might just make her change her mind about selling!"

"We'd best get going then!" Jock said, looking at Alice who was pale and jittery.

But at that moment they saw the back of a trailer roll towards of the exit of the racetrack with a dun pony's rump and tail just visible inside. Within seconds it disappeared from sight. The five of them ran to Jock's Land Rover and jumped in. But Jock was parked furthest away from the exit, and as they pulled out they got stuck in a snaking queue of trailers all converging towards it at the same time.

After what seemed like for ever Jock was finally roaring away from the racetrack. There were horse trailers everywhere, almost all of them being towed by Range Rovers or Land Rovers – they all looked the same!

"We've lost her!" Alice said, starting to panic. "What do we do now?"

"Trouble is, there are lots of different roads Mrs Valentine could take to get back to your neck of the woods," Jock said, leaning forward over the wheel, nose pressed to the window and his foot down hard. "And there's no knowing which one she'd have taken."

Everyone fell into an intense silence, racking their brains for a plan.

"I've got it!" Mia suddenly exclaimed. "It's obvious! Mrs Valentine won't be going straight home – she'll be dropping off the dun pony first. And we know exactly where that'll be if the pattern's the same as before, don't we?"

Alice, Charlie and Rosie looked at each other as they bumped about in the back of the jeep, holding on to whatever they could.

"Dragonfly Marsh!" they all cried, breaking into smiles.

"Yes!" Mia replied. "We can cut her off there!"

"Ah, now though," Jock explained apologetically, "I need to be at my next job straight after I get back. It's at two o'clock."

"I know! If you drop us back at Blackberry Farm," Charlie said, all fired up, "we can ride over to the marsh and then catch Mrs Valentine there as she drops off the dun pony!"

Jock looked anxious. "Well, if you really *have* to, but make sure you ring me straightaway if you run into any trouble. Deal?"

The girls agreed excitedly, knowing that the chase was back on. They sat on the edge of their seats, willing Jock to get back as fast as his Land Rover could carry them.

Chapter Twelve

As soon as they came to a halt at Blackberry Farm they leaped out of the Land Rover, shouting their thanks and goodbyes to Jock, who told them to hurry. He called out good luck as the doors slammed and the girls raced to the tack room. The ponies were already in their stables as Rosie had called her mum earlier to ask if, on this one occasion, she could bring them in from the paddock and give them some hay.

Dancer looked rather taken aback as Rosie rushed into her stable, giving her a quick kiss and a hug before she had the briefest of flick-overs and was tacked up. The strawberry roan mulishly left her stable, her head stretched out, not enjoying all the rush around her, as the others brought their ponies out onto the yard and jumped into the saddles. Even Beanie looked bewildered as Rosie raced past, patting his soft head briefly before she lifted Dancer's saddle flap to tighten the girth.

"Just this once," Rosie said as her mare stubbornly puffed herself out on purpose, "I need you to sprout wings and not be on a go-slow day..."

Rosie led her to the concrete mounting block, closing the yard gate behind her after the others had all jogged out, and climbed on board. Pirate, sensing that they were on a mission, was already cantering on the spot, and as soon as Charlie relaxed her hands slightly he burst forward, with Scout jogging just behind. Wish strode out and even Dancer sensed their urgency and didn't do her usual loitering by the gate but followed the others quickly, a surprised look in her goggly eyes.

They trotted briskly along the track, out onto Duck Lane, then turned off on the first bridleway, cantering every bit that they could, even if it was only for a few strides through the woods, until they reached an open field and let the ponies fly. When they reached the end, Alice glanced over her shoulder as she pulled up and saw Wish right behind her and Dancer not far off, a look of pink determination on Rosie's face.

Charlie glanced at her watch. Jock had driven as fast as his jeep would allow, which hadn't been all that fast, but she could guarantee that a car and trailer with a pony loaded would be slower. Even so, they'd be cutting it fine to get across to the marsh in time. She pressed a willing Pirate on and he took off once they'd got through the next gate and had shut it behind them.

The others flew after him, with Wish excited by the chase and enjoying herself as she raced alongside Scout, who had his head down, galloping fast. Alice and Mia were out of their saddles, tucked low like jockeys on their ponies' backs. Dancer was only a few strides behind as they thundered across the long, open, undulating field. At the end of it they pulled up and rode out onto a lane. They walked the ponies along in tense silence. They knew that they had to get to Dragonfly Marsh in time to catch Mrs Valentine unloading lot 107, so that they could tell her everything they knew, but the ponies needed a quick break too.

"Everyone ready?" Charlie asked up at the front after they'd been walking quickly for a while, turning in the saddle to see how the others were doing. They all nodded back and Charlie popped Pirate back into trot, the ponies' rhythmical hoof beats echoing on the lane between the overhanging leafy trees. Suddenly they ducked off onto a bridleway and found themselves on a path alongside some ancient, dilapidated post-and-rail fencing. Beyond that lay Dragonfly Marsh.

They cantered the last bit, riding along the fence line until they got near to the gate where Mrs Valentine would have to unload the dun pony.

The landscape had opened up, with the flat marsh stretching to the right of them, so they could see for what felt like miles. And that's when they noticed the puff of dust and just saw in the midst of it a trailer. The only trouble was, it wasn't heading in the direction of the gate, but away from it. And there, standing nervously in front of them, was lot 107 with the sticker still stuck on his rump.

"We're too late!" Rosie cried desperately, collapsing on Dancer's neck as they reached the dun. He neighed and rushed forward, poking his head over the gate to meet them and looking grateful for the company.

Mia watched as the puff of dust slowly snaked into the distance.

"I've got to follow her," Alice suddenly said. Her insides, which had been tied in knots on the way over, suddenly started somersaulting at the thought, but she didn't have a choice, Scout's future hung in the balance and she'd do anything to keep him. Mia pulled their map out of her saddle pouch. They quickly flipped it open, turned it round and studied it.

"Look, the track Mrs Valentine is driving along goes right around the edge of the marsh before it comes out onto a little lane," Charlie said. "If we ride straight across the marsh, we've still got a chance of cutting her off!"

Rosie looked as worried as the dun.

"I'm not being funny but I don't know that Dancer will make it across there," she said seriously. The marsh was uneven, with tall reeds and marsh grasses. There were paths but they were fairly narrow, criss-crossing across the boggy land. If they came off the paths, who knows what they might be sploshing about in? It made Rosie shiver just thinking about it. "Dancer could end up being swallowed by the bog. And what if we got lost? We might still be riding round at midnight!"

"Er, it's a marsh, Rosie, not a swamp," Charlie reminded her, but Rosie wasn't convinced.

"I know! Why don't me and Rosie stay here while you two both ride across?" Mia suddenly suggested. "That way we split up, but Dancer doesn't have to wait here on her own."

"Perfect! Charlie, what do you reckon?" Alice asked, knowing they couldn't hang around talking about it much longer; they had to get going. "I can go on my own if you'd rather not come?"

"Try and stop me," Charlie smiled, pushing her hat onto her head.

Alice felt a rush of relief at not having to go it alone, grateful that Charlie and Pirate were both fearless. She opened the gate and rode through it, leaving the safety of the path. Scout stepped lightly onto the vastness of Dragonfly Marsh.

Mia jumped out of the saddle and handed her reins to Rosie. She followed Charlie and Alice off the path into the marsh and clicked shut the gate behind them. Then she pulled the belt off her jodhpurs and slipped it over the dun pony's neck, holding both the ends so she could keep him with her and Rosie, rather than let him race loose after Charlie and Alice. Mia watched as Scout and Pirate jogged along the narrow track which was just about visible, before they disappeared into a dip, ducking out of sight below the level of the tallest reeds.

Charlie kept Pirate tucked in just behind Scout, following his every hoof print in the soft ground. Alice swallowed hard as she popped Scout into a steady canter. His ears were pricked and it was clear that he remembered Dragonfly Marsh from his time being turned out on there the summer before, confident in his footing as he dodged through the tall reeds. Alice let his pace increase, calling over her shoulder to check that Charlie was okay. Charlie shouted out that she was fine.

Like Alice, she was hovering out of the saddle, holding a handful of mane so that Pirate had his head to help him balance. Charlie stretched out her fingers on one hand and scratched his withers, watching his ears flicker briefly before he turned his attention back to the narrow path ahead, ignoring the mud spatters thrown up by Scout's hooves.

All the time they cantered fast, whipping between the reeds, Alice kept one eye over to the left on the little cloud of dust, watching Mrs Valentine's slow progress along the higher track around the edge of the boggy marsh. Every now and again she disappeared from view as the ground dipped down so that all Alice could see were the tall, dry reeds like a wall on either side of her. She trusted completely in the sure-footed Scout and she half closed her eyes, raising her arm every now and again to brush aside the reeds if they blew too close. It was just after she'd opened her eyes again that she heard a squeal behind her.

She turned quickly, just in time to see that Pirate had stumbled. Charlie had tipped forward and was clinging onto his neck, hanging precariously to the side. Alice sat back in her saddle.

"Whoa, steady Scout," she called as she squeezed on his reins.

He came back to a bouncy canter, then to a trot. Alice glanced round just as Charlie slipped to the ground. She landed on her feet in a boggy puddle with a splosh. Pirate jogged to Scout, barging into his rump. Alice was terrified that he was going to scrape past and go flying off across the marsh, not knowing where he was headed, and with stirrups and reins flying everywhere. She swiftly leaned across and grabbed his reins, but she realised as Charlie ran up to him that he was sticking by Scout and not going anywhere.

"Are you okay?" Alice asked as she watched Charlie flip her offside stirrup back over the saddle. Charlie nodded, smiling ruefully.

"I was so busy watching the dust cloud that

I forgot to look where I was going," she said, jumping back into the saddle.

"The track's starting to curve back towards us," Alice noticed as Charlie got her stirrups and they set off again at a fast trot, "and that must mean that we're nearly at the other side. I just hope we find a gate to the lane quickly!"

The ponies picked up canter again and they threaded their way through the reeds, ducking left and right, and keeping to the raised path until the reeds started to thin out. The dust cloud was getting nearer, and they could hear the car engine with the clatter of the trailer rattling behind it. Alice noticed some fencing just ahead as the car drew level with them. She bobbed down low in the saddle, taking cover in what reeds were left around them as Scout fell back to trot. The car drove past. It picked up speed as it left the bumpy track and reached a smooth-surfaced lane. Alice looked around wildly.

"There isn't a gate!" she panicked. "How are we meant to follow her?!"

Charlie looked ahead, keeping her eyes fixed on the trailer bumping off into the distance. She watched helplessly as it indicated left, then turned between a break in the hedge and disappeared out of sight. Her shoulders slumped.

"We can't lose her now, not after all this," Alice groaned, her legs aching from standing in the stirrups for so long. She could tell that after their epic ride Scout was starting to feel tired beneath her too.

Suddenly she heard the engine stop. Not like it was going out of earshot but as if it had been switched off. Without hesitating, she flung herself out of the saddle. Charlie grabbed Scout's reins, caught by surprise, as Alice clambered over the wooden fence and started to sprint up the lane, making for the gap in the hedge.

Her legs were like lead and it felt as if she was treading water, but the thought of catching Mrs Valentine spurred her on. She slowed gratefully at the edge of the gap. Before ducking round it, she parted the hedge. There stood the sleek Range Rover and the trailer, parked right next to a huge, ultra-smart caravan that was tucked away to the side out of sight. At that second, she looked across and caught a glimpse of someone stepping into the caravan. Suddenly, her phone vibrated. Glad she'd remembered to switch it to silent, she quickly grabbed it and answered it with shaking breath.

"What's happening?" Charlie whispered.

"I've found the trailer and I just saw someone heading into a caravan!" Alice whispered back.

"Someone? You mean Mrs Valentine, right?" Charlie asked, lying along Pirate's neck, craning to see.

"Well, I only saw their leg, so I can't be a hundred per cent sure," Alice replied hesitantly. "I'll have to get a bit closer."

Alice tiptoed around the hedge and up the rubble drive. She crept past the empty trailer and the Range Rover, her heart thumping as the rubble crunched beneath each step. She looked up and saw someone appear for a second at the window of the caravan. Alice ducked behind the trailer as the woman inside peered out then drew the curtain. As the lights inside the caravan flickered on, Alice frowned, confused suddenly – something didn't add up.

She was hiding behind the same trailer that had dropped off the pony which Mrs Valentine had bought, the trailer they'd followed from the other side of the marsh. But the person she'd seen in the window of the caravan was *not* Mrs Valentine. This woman's hair was definitely *not* long and blonde.

"But we saw the trailer come in here," Alice said quietly to herself, "the same trailer that dropped off the dun pony. It has to be the right one, so where is Mrs Valentine?"

Alice crept forward. She needed to try to get another peek inside the caravan – she needed to work out what was going on. As she edged past the Range Rover, something inside caught her eye. There, lying on the passenger seat were a pair of large, dark sunglasses, a wide-brimmed hat, and a long blonde wig.

Alice felt her heart skip a beat. Suddenly, the last thing she wanted to do was go up and confront the woman in the caravan. What she really wanted to do was turn tail and run, but instead she reached for her phone with shaking fingers. She opened up the camera and quickly took a couple of shots of the hat and wig, knowing that's what Mia would do, before flying back up the lane.

"What happened?" Charlie whispered as Alice raced towards her. "Did you speak to Mrs Valentine?"

Alice hastily climbed the fence. She grabbed her reins then swung lightly back into the saddle.

"That's not Mrs Valentine!" she whispered, puffing.

"What do you mean?" Charlie asked, looking

surprised. "That was the same trailer we know dropped off the dun pony – it has to be her!"

Alice shook her head, almost too excited and nervous at her discovery to talk.

"No, I mean, I think it *is* Mrs Valentine, at least, the person who's been *pretending* to be Mrs Valentine," Alice said, almost getting more muddled as she tried to make sense of it, "but that's just a disguise! She's been wearing a wig, glasses and a hat all along, since the first time I met her last year! Anyway, look, we can't hang around here – we have to go!"

The girls quickly turned their ponies then disappeared back into the long marsh grasses.

"So who is she?" Charlie asked impatiently, once they were safely hidden from the lane.

"Well, under the wig she's got short, black hair," Alice revealed, letting Scout's reins go loose. "I can't be a hundred per cent definite before I check the photo in the newspaper, but I'm pretty sure I know who it is."

"I don't believe it!" Charlie said, slapping her mud-splattered hat as she worked it out.

Alice nodded.

"Mrs Hawk!"

Chapter Thirteen

AFTER walking Scout and Pirate back across the seemingly endless marsh, they finally reached the fencing at the other side. Charlie had called ahead to update Rosie and Mia, who were still waiting on the path by the gate. They'd taken Dancer's and Wish's saddles off and let their ponies graze the other side of the fence from the nervy dun pony. When Alice and Charlie finally rode into sight, Mia held the gate open for them, being careful not to let the dun pony out. They felt terrible leaving him behind, but they hoped that he wouldn't now be alone on Dragonfly Marsh for long. As the four rode back to Blackberry Farm, Alice and Charlie filled Mia and Rosie in properly. As soon as they'd reached the yard and untacked,

Rosie rushed to get the old newspaper article.

"It was *definitely* Mrs Hawk!" Alice cried, studying it closely. "The woman in the caravan was the spitting image of the woman in the picture here!"

"One thing's for sure, the name Hawk suits her *way* better than 'Valentine' ever did!" Rosie puffed.

"And no wonder her hair always looked like straw," Mia said critically. "That wig was *not* great quality."

"That's hardly the most important fact right now," Charlie commented as they all walked over to the barn with their nets, stuffing them full of sweet-smelling, soft hay before carrying them back to the yard for the ponies to eat while the girls groomed them.

"No," Mia agreed. "The most important fact is that Mrs Hawk has been banned from keeping ponies, but she's found what she thought was a sneaky way round it."

"And I bet that's why she moved Scout to Dragonfly Marsh after her moonlight flit from Hollow Hill!" Alice burst out. "He was the first pony Jock noticed marshy hooves on, so that's when she must have switched from being Mrs Hawk to being Mrs Valentine."

"Exactly!" Charlie said as she heaved on the haynet to pull it as high as it could go before tying it up to the baler twine on the ring outside Pirate's stable. He tucked in greedily, hungry after the long ride. "The marsh is so big, the ponies could almost get lost out there. It's the perfect place to hide ponies you've been banned from owning!"

"And as well as hiding her ponies on the marsh," Rosie continued, "she moved away from her cottage at Hollow Hill, changed her name *and* her appearance..."

"... and carried on buying ponies with Roger Green's help," Charlie said crossly. "Only since her ban she put them out on loan rather than keeping them on Hollow Common."

"And it meant she could keep the fact that she still owned ponies a secret," Alice sighed, giving Scout lots of mints. "After all, anyone coming to try the ponies would have to try the pony at the loan home, rather than at Mrs Hawk's."

She turned on the yard tap and sluiced buckets of warm water over his neck, back and legs, rinsing off all the mud and dried, crinkled sweat before splashing her own face and drying it on her T-shirt. Charlie did the same. Mia watched in horror as Charlie left long mud streaks smeared across her T-shirt without a care.

"Clever, really," Rosie said, giving Dancer a hug, "but not clever enough to fool the Pony Detectives."

"So what do we do now?" Alice asked.

"There's a number for the RSPCA on the article," Mia said, picking up the cutting once more as Wish shook her head then rubbed the side of her nose against an outstretched foreleg.

Mia took her phone out of her pocket and

dialled the number, checking it against the paper. She was put on hold, and paced up and down the yard until she was put through to someone and could explain their discovery: that the banned Mrs Hawk still owned ponies, even though they were out on loan. She also mentioned that Mrs Hawk had just bought a dun pony who'd been turned out on Dragonfly Marsh all alone.

"You'll come out? Brilliant!" Mia said excitedly. Then her face dropped. "Oh, is that the soonest you can make it? It's just that Mrs Val—I mean, Mrs *Hawk*'s due to come here tomorrow at three o'clock. She's planning to sell on one of the ponies she's not even meant to own, and she might be gone by the time you get here..."

Mia gave the address for Blackberry Farm before ending the call.

"So?" Alice asked, her stomach in a tight knot.

"The earliest they think they'll be able to make it is four tomorrow," Mia explained, taking a deep breath, "but they've said that they'll definitely try

to make it earlier, especially as it would mean finally catching up with Mrs Hawk."

"But Tallulah's dad's due at three o'clock – Scout will be sold by then!" Alice gasped. It felt as if, however hard they tried, Scout's safety was always an infuriating step away.

"We'll just have to try to keep Mrs Hawk here until they come," Charlie said, frowning.

"Or we could put a back-up plan into action to stop Tallulah buying Scout. Me and Rosie came up with one while we were waiting for you two this afternoon," Mia said quickly, "just in case you lost Mrs Hawk across the marsh. It's all set up – we just need Tallulah to appear today like she said she would and then I'll send one text..."

At that moment they heard a car on the bumpy drive, then footsteps. A second later Tallulah was bouncing into the yard, all smug smiles and superiority until she saw Scout, his pink skin showing through his silky wet coat.

"What are you doing to my pony?" she squealed

as Scout shook himself, his hooves scraping slightly on the concrete. She rushed back, wiping the water off her smart top as if it was infected.

"Er, washing him down?" Alice said, wondering how she'd have reacted if she'd been on the yard five minutes earlier when Scout had been covered in mud. She glanced across to Mia and Rosie who were both looking as smug as Tallulah. They hadn't had time to explain the plan to her or Charlie, so she'd just have to trust them, she thought, as she noticed Mia fiddling with the mobile phone in her pocket. "Anyway, he's not your pony yet."

Tallulah shrugged her shoulders.

"As good as. As it goes, I don't mind if you're washing him. It'll just make him look even better for the show on Saturday."

At that moment, Mia's mobile phone started to ring. She answered it after the first ring, putting it on speaker phone.

"Mia?" The voice at the other end rang out. "It's Poppy!"

Mia smiled, watching out of the corner of her eye as Tallulah suddenly perked up and shamelessly listened in.

"Listen," Poppy continued. "I know that Scout's as good as sold, but I just really wanted to jump him before it all goes through. It might be my last chance and I'd love to find out what feel he gives me over a fence and how he compares to Moonlight."

"Of course – I know Alice won't mind!" Mia replied, smiling to herself as Rosie nudged Alice in the ribs and Alice called out that she didn't mind in the slightest. "How about ten o'clock tomorrow morning? I'll get some jumps set up for you."

"Great," Poppy said. "Make sure they're big ones, won't you?"

"Will do," Mia said, before they said their goodbyes.

"What is Poppy Brookes doing calling you about *my* pony?" Tallulah asked indignantly.

"I guess she just wants to find out what she's missed out on," Rosie replied. "She was really impressed with his performance in the Eventers Grand Prix last weekend."

"I *knew* I'd made the right decision about buying Shooting Starr. It's so brilliant that I've bought him and she hasn't!" Tallulah squealed excitedly. "She'll be so jealous after she rides him tomorrow and realises that even Moonlight's no match for him! What time did you say she's coming down tomorrow? Ten?"

Mia nodded, and Tallulah marched out of the yard looking more smug than ever. As they heard a car door slam shut and Tallulah whizzed up the lane with her mum, Mia and Rosie quickly brought Charlie and Alice up to speed. The four girls collapsed into giggles. Their plan was in place. Now they just needed it to work.

Chapter Fourteen

"ALL set?" Poppy smiled as she tightened Scout's girth. She'd mounted him in the little yard where Moonlight was safely housed in the spare stable and pressed him forward into a walk as she lowered her leg and the saddle flap. Alice walked by Scout's head with Mia on the other side. Charlie and Rosie were already in the schooling paddock, dragging the ancient, peeling show-jumping poles, with their scraps of red, blue and green paint, across the dusty ring.

Mia nodded as they headed down past the turn-out paddock, into the shade of the tall, overhanging trees and then in through the squeaky metal gate to the schooling area.

Scout strode out keenly into the ring, his ears pricked as he looked around. Alice could see that he was happy with Poppy on his back, like a completely different pony compared to when Tallulah had been in the saddle.

Mia sat on a barrel laid on its side next to Alice, while Rosie and Charlie took up position next to them. Suddenly, there was a flurry of straightened hair, glittery eyeshadow and brightly coloured T-shirt and jodhpurs.

"Hi guys!" Tallulah said, walking fast over to the ring. "Mum was going to come and watch today too, only she's making important calls in the car right now. She's getting the money sorted for the handover with Mrs Valentine this afternoon. I told her I want this sale to go smoothly. Oh, hi, Poppy! I see you're up on my new superstar! Doesn't he feel gorgeous?!"

"Feels okay so far. I'll warm him up first."

Poppy smiled as she moved Scout into a trot after walking him on a long rein to loosen him up. "Then I'll let you know once I've popped him over some big fences."

Poppy winked quickly at Alice as she rode past. Alice held her hand up to her mouth to hide her smile. She knew that Poppy had no intention of getting to the point of jumping any big fences on Scout. Their plan would be well finished before it got to that stage.

Alice watched as Poppy had Scout moving brilliantly. But every now and again, just as he was going well, she'd half-halt him, then tip forward.

"Is he looking a bit lame to you?" Poppy called out.

The others made a show of checking Scout's trot, but they decided that, if he was, it must be intermittent. Poppy tipped forward a few more times, then turned him to the cross pole, the lowest of the six fences set up around the schooling paddock. He jumped it eagerly and, after a few times over it, Poppy asked for it to be raised.

This time she turned him to it in a canter but, a few strides before the fence, she pulled Scout up, paused for a second, then reined him back, getting him to step backwards at an angle from the fence. Alice had to smile to herself. She knew exactly what Poppy was doing because they'd set it up beforehand, as they'd sat quietly together in the tack room. Alice knew that Poppy had asked Scout to stop properly and had performed a good rein-back. Only to someone watching who didn't know any better, from the way Poppy had acted in the saddle they'd have thought that Scout was playing up, refusing to go near the fence.

Tallulah frowned.

"Is he often like this?" Poppy asked, sounding frustrated and impatient. Tallulah turned to look at Alice crossly, as if it was all her fault.

"He can be," Alice replied apologetically, glancing at Tallulah. "He's been like it a bit more recently."

“Maybe you’ve over-faced him,” Poppy replied, “taking him over fences that are too big for him. I’ll try him again, but he hasn’t got that forward-going feel of a pony who really takes you into a fence, one that you know will always jump when you get there, no matter what’s in front of you, like Moonlight does. That’s the sign of a true star.”

With each comment Tallulah glowered more darkly at Alice, her nostrils flaring furiously.

Poppy jumped Scout a few more times, setting Scout up expertly on a stride that took him in close to the fence, then asking him to stand off, but not once getting him to do anything that would have scared him. It was just her antics in the saddle which made the jumps look erratic. Each time, she grimaced or purposely lost a stirrup or almost fell off sideways out of the saddle.

“Scout’s jumping technique’s really odd,” she commented, bringing Scout back to a walk. “It’s really hard to predict what kind of jump he’s going to make, so it's difficult for me to ride into the fences with any confidence. Weird!"

Tallulah's face turned pink. She glared once more at Alice, who had to turn away so Tallulah couldn't see her smile.

"Let's put it up a bit," Poppy said. "Although if he's as inconsistent as that over the small fences, I doubt he'll be any better over the bigger ones to be honest. But it's worth a go – I might be wrong."

Rosie and Charlie rushed over to the fence, slid out the metal cups and slotted the pins in three holes higher.

Poppy turned into the bigger fence. This time she tucked Scout in close to the fence and tipped forward, landing as if she was about to fall off the side. Poppy made a show of only just clinging on to the saddle before pulling him up. As she did, she tipped forward once more.

"Are you *sure* he's not a bit lame?" she asked, looking down at his off fore as she rode over to the centre of the school. "Maybe it's all the jumping catching up with him. It might be that he hasn't got the strongest tendons."

Tallulah's eyebrows disappeared under her fringe. She fumed so violently that Rosie worried that she was in danger of exploding.

"Did you want to try him over a course?" Mia asked, standing up. "We put the other fences up specially."

"Erm, actually I don't think I'll bother," Poppy replied, patting Scout then swinging her leg over and jumping down. She immediately bent over to run her hand over the tendons on Scout's off fore before looking up at Alice and passing her Scout's reins. "Oh well, I'm glad I've tried him. You never know, maybe I just caught him on a bad day."

Poppy smiled, but she didn't sound convinced.

"Well, we all know he can jump," Tallulah said defiantly as Alice led Scout back to the yard. "Maybe you just didn't click with him like I did. Because I ride so many ponies, I can normally strike up a partnership pretty quickly."

Alice looked nervously across to Mia, who made a bit of a face until she saw Tallulah looking at her suspiciously. She changed it quickly into a smile, feeling her olive skin flush slightly as if she'd been caught out. She seriously hoped that Tallulah wouldn't work out what was going on.

As soon as they got back to the yard, Poppy made a fuss about tacking Moonlight back up and getting going.

"I've got loads of tack cleaning to do tomorrow ahead of the show," she groaned, "so I better get back. I guess I'll see you in the Sweetbriar Cup, Tallulah."

"I'll be there, although I've got such a good team of ponies I haven't actually decided which one I'll enter yet," she replied, showing off.

"Oh, right," Poppy said, before turning to Alice. "Let me know if you want any help finding a real jumper for your next pony. I'm sure I can find you one with more scope and ability than Scout."

At that, Tallulah gasped slightly. Then she flounced across the yard and seconds later roared up the drive in her mum's car. As she disappeared, the others all looked at each other.

"Do you think I've done enough?" Poppy whispered.

"I guess we'll just have to wait and see now," Mia sighed. It was impossible to tell if Tallulah really believed she was a better jockey than Poppy, or if she had been put off Scout by the fact that Poppy pretended not to rate him any more.

"Well, we don't have long now to wait before we find out," Charlie said, as Poppy got Moonlight tacked up and led him out of the spare stable.

"Good luck, Alice," she said, looking over with a bright smile, hoping to make Alice feel confident. "At least you know you've done everything possible. Just a question of fingers crossed now!"

Alice nodded, a feeling worse than entering fifty huge shows suddenly coursing through her and making her shiver. She turned and hugged

Scout, then checked her watch. Mrs Hawk was due in just under three hours. It sounded like nothing, but she knew it would be the longest and most nerve-racking three hours of her life. She just had no idea which way Tallulah would go. None of them did.

Chapter Fifteen

ALICE felt sick. She'd heard the car on the track and felt her knees buckle, thinking that it was Tallulah's horsebox. When Rosie, being lookout again at the gate, had called out that Mrs Hawk had arrived, her sickness turned to a twist of nerves as she thought about what was about to happen. She willed the RSPCA Inspector to turn up, but Rosie kept reporting that there were no other sightings, making her heart sink down into her boots as Mrs Hawk stalked onto the yard. If Mrs Hawk was here she knew it meant that Tallulah hadn't called to cancel the sale. And that meant that their plan that morning must have failed. The RSPCA was Alice's last hope, but so far they were nowhere in sight.

Mrs Hawk stopped by Scout's stable and looked over the door. Alice had spent the last three hours glued to his side, hugging him, grooming him, plaiting and unplaiting his mane, but mainly just leaning against him, whispering with a nervous, shaky voice as she told him that he wouldn't be going anywhere. She'd hugged him as he rubbed his head against her.

Suddenly, as badly as she'd wanted her dreams to come true, the cold, unbending reality pushed its way into her thoughts: that very soon she could be standing in an empty stable and Scout would be on a strange yard, not knowing any of the smells, the noises or the people or ponies around him. Alice had wanted desperately for time to stand still, but it wouldn't. She'd tried, but as the clock ticked closer to three, she could no longer hold back all the fear that had been racing around in her mind for the past week and hot tears started to spill down her cheeks.

She'd heard the bolt on her door go and turned to see Rosie, Charlie and Mia standing next to her. Rosie had put her arms around her and Mia had told her with a wobbly voice that somehow it would all work out all right. Alice had nodded, wanting desperately to believe her, but somewhere deep in her heart her unfailing belief was starting to feel shaken. She was worried that everything was happening too late.

She'd blown her nose just as Rosie had gone to be lookout and Charlie and Mia had gone to check on their ponies. Two minutes later, Mrs Hawk had arrived.

"Glad to see you've made him look half decent," Mrs Hawk commented as she glanced over the door, her wig and hat back in place, along with the sunglasses.

"Not that there's much point," Rosie muttered under her breath as she strode over, "because he's not going anywhere."

"What was that?" Mrs Hawk asked irritably,

looking at her watch and tutting as it ticked to five past three.

"I said he won't be going anywhere," Rosie repeated louder. Alice felt her insides twist as she saw Mia and Charlie heading towards the stable. They'd agreed that if the RSPCA Inspector didn't show up they'd confront Mrs Hawk themselves before Tallulah got there. It looked as if the others were just about ready.

"What are you talking about?" Mrs Hawk scoffed. "As soon as Tallulah's dad turns up with the cash that grey will be out of this wretched little place."

"But we know your secret," Mia said, standing on one side of Scout's stable with the others, while Mrs Hawk stood on the other.

"Hmm? What secret's that?" Mrs Hawk asked distractedly, checking her watch again.

"How Roger Green keeps prices low on certain ponies at his auctions," Mia continued, taking a deep breath as she saw Mrs Hawk stiffen slightly,

"then you buy them with his help. You loan them out and sell them on for a big, fat profit, which you split with the auctioneer."

Mrs Hawk lowered her glasses for a second, looking at Mia with beady eyes, her anger glowing.

"Rather clever of me, don't you think?" she gloated. "Anyway, it's not against the law."

"No, but owning ponies when you've been banned is," Mia replied. "Mrs *Hawk*!"

"Ha!" Rosie cried, pointing her finger in the air.

Mia nudged her.

"What? I didn't know what else to say, and I wanted to add my bit!" Rosie whispered back as Mrs Hawk stood for a second, her thin lips curling into a slow smile.

"We know everything," Mia continued, showing her the newspaper article. Mrs Hawk reached to grab it, her wig twisting sideways, but Mia flicked the paper out of her grasp just in time.

Mrs Hawk still looked annoyingly triumphant,

although Alice noticed a bead of sweat form on her top lip. "Oh, do carry on. Tell me what you think you know," she sneered.

"We went to try to find you at the address in Hollow Hill that you gave Alice." Charlie cleared her throat, thrown by a hard stare from Mrs Hawk. "We didn't find you but we did find Beth Bright. She led us to Sammy, who told us you bought Scout at an auction at a knock-down price. Then we heard the phone call from 'R', Roger Green, and followed you to his auction, where we found out about your deal with the auctioneer."

"And we worked out the link between all the ponies on the marsh," Alice continued, "so we called the owners and found that you'd told everyone the same story. And before you ask, we've got evidence – of you talking to Roger Green, and your wig."

"You had to wear a disguise so that no one recognised you," Mia added, "once you'd been banned."

"But you couldn't fool the Pony Detectives," Rosie said triumphantly.

Mrs Hawk lowered her sunglasses to look at the four girls. For a fleeting second there was a flash of admiration in her eyes before they turned steely again.

"Oh, you may think you've got one over on me, but I've managed to escape detection this long and I don't intend being caught now. Especially not by four interfering girls – the Pony Detectives, indeed!" Mrs Hawk chuckled gleefully to herself. "Anyway, as interesting as all this is, if it's a ploy to get me to sell Scout to you, it won't work. As soon as Tallulah turns up, I'm grabbing the cash and disappearing. Very soon no one will know where I am or what disguise I'm wearing next, except me and Roger. So it really doesn't matter what you know – it'll make no difference the moment I drive away from this lousy yard."

Alice opened her mouth, holding Scout. At that second a phone rang. It was Mrs Hawk's.

"Ah, that's Tallulah's dad now," Mrs Hawk smiled thinly, "no doubt telling me they're on their way. This will all be over in a short while, and this pony and I will be nothing more than a distant memory."

Mrs Hawk took the call. The girls could hear Tallulah's dad ranting in the background, but couldn't make out any of the words. But they didn't need to: Mrs Hawk's twisted face said all they needed to know.

"What do you mean, no good at jumping? He's been coming first all summer! Anyway, we had a deal!" she fumed. "I've cancelled my advert in *Pony Mad* because of you – you can't just change your mind now, it's too late! Hello... hello?"

Mrs Hawk stared at her phone incredulously. She frowned, reached for Scout's stable door and swung it open furiously. Rosie looked up and nudged Charlie and Mia, who glanced over to the track beyond the cottage and smiled secretly to each other.

"That's it!" Mrs Hawk exclaimed, grabbing at Scout's lead rope. "I'm off, and before you go getting any ideas about keeping this pony, he's coming with me!"

But as Mrs Hawk dragged Scout out of his stable a car door slammed and a man and a woman walked in through the gate and marched straight up to her. They were both wearing uniforms with peaked caps, and had RSPCA logos on their tops.

"Going somewhere, Mrs Hawk?"

For the first time, Mrs Hawk looked alarmed. She was cornered. She glanced furtively around the yard, beads of sweat rolling down her face as she desperately searched for an escape route. The only one was right past the Inspectors. She seemed to sense that she was defeated and, with sagging shoulders, she dropped the lead rope and accompanied them to the tack room. Alice quickly took hold of the rope, patting a slightly confused Scout before taking him back to his stable.

The four girls waited till Mrs Hawk had disappeared into the tack room with the Inspectors, then crept up and stood by the door, straining to hear Mrs Hawk's responses as the Inspectors produced some paperwork and asked her to sign it.

"What is it?" she croaked suspiciously.

"This is to sign over every pony you currently own to us," the woman said, "including the grey on this yard and the three others you have out on loan. Then there's the dun pony from the marsh, which we've got in the back of our trailer right now."

Mrs Hawk grumbled under her breath and the girls heard her muttering about them being busybodies before she snatched the pen from the man and scrawled her name on the page held out to her.

"So what does that mean?" Alice whispered, turning anxiously to the others, suddenly panicking that Scout might get loaded into the trailer with the rescued dun. "What happens to Scout now?"

At that moment the RSPCA Inspectors came out and led Mrs Hawk to their car.

"Excuse me..." Alice cleared her throat, going pink as the man turned back to her. "It's just that I've got a pony on loan from Mrs Hawk, the grey over there... what's going to happen to him? Will he have to be taken away?"

Alice felt her heart flip as he smiled at her kindly.

"Well, now we've got him signed over to us, along with the others which we'll locate," the man explained, "we'll start the process of rehoming the ponies which are in good enough condition."

"Rehoming...?" Alice said, her voice sticking in her throat. Her eyes prickled and her vision blurred at the thought that her saviours were about to become the ones to finally take Scout away from her.

"With someone suitable and knowledgeable," the man said seriously, "someone who can offer the pony a forever home, who'll promise to love the pony for its whole life."

Alice nodded, looking at a yellow dandelion on the floor which danced and smudged in front of her eyes as a big teardrop rolled down her face and landed on it.

"We have to check that the stables are safe. And although the pony officially is always owned by us, we have to make sure that the person taking the pony is dedicated to having him on long-term, permanent loan," the man continued, looking round at Blackberry Farm's yard. "And this, to me, looks like just the kind of place that I'd be looking for."

Alice nodded again. Then she heard Rosie gasp, and Mia and Charlie start to laugh, slightly hysterically. She looked up. The man was looking at her, smiling so that his eyes had almost disappeared in all the crinkles on his face. Alice glanced round at the others, not able to catch her breath for a second.

"Do you... do you mean...?" Alice looked at the man, who was the one nodding now. She burst out laughing but it came out as a huge sob and she suddenly heard someone squeal and realised it was her. The others all hugged her, bouncing up and down on the spot.

"I'm happy that keeping this pony here with you is the best outcome for him," the man said, laughing too. "There'll be paperwork and proper checks for us to complete but we can do that after we've sorted out Mrs Hawk. I'll pop back tomorrow."

With that he turned and walked over to his car. Alice stood, stunned for a second, before rushing over to Scout's stable. She let herself in and hugged him, patting him over and over, kissing his muzzle and, with shaking fingers, finding him mints.

"Did you hear that, Scout?" Alice whispered through big gulps. "I promise to look after you and love you for ever, and there's *nothing* now that will ever, ever keep us apart."

Scout rested his chin on Alice's shoulder, his warm breath fluffing her hair as he blinked his eyes softly. Alice knew then that he finally really was hers and that her biggest dream had just come true.

Chapter Sixteen

Alice couldn't stop grinning as she waited just outside one of the roped-off rings at the Sweetbriar Stud show. It was the last show of the summer holidays and the paddocks were filled with milling crowds and dogs barking in the bright September sunshine. Rosie had persuaded them to forget about serious jumping or showing competitions for once. After the week they'd had, she'd suggested that they ought to just have some fun instead. The others had totally agreed. Alice sighed happily. The RSPCA Inspector had arrived at the yard that morning first thing and her parents had joined them there. They'd gone through all the documents and paperwork, just like the Inspector had promised they would. Alice felt the happiness bubble up inside her. Scout was finally, officially on loan to her – for ever – *and* the Pony Detectives had successfully solved their second mystery.

She heard a high-pitched cough and looked up. Tallulah Starr, looking as smart as ever on her patient grey pony, Diamond Starr, stood in front of her.

"So, you've decided not to enter for the Cup, I see," Tallulah scoffed, looking at the ring for fun classes that Alice was waiting by. "I am, of course, but I'm not surprised that you're in *this* class. More on your pony's level, I guess. I mean, he hasn't got the *scope* that I'd be looking for in a top-class jumper – I'd get rid of him if I were you."

Alice smiled to herself. After all, her love for Scout had nothing to do with how high or how wide he could jump. But Alice didn't bother to try explaining that to Tallulah; somehow Alice knew that she'd never understand.

At that moment, Poppy rode past on Moonlight. She'd called Alice the evening before to find out the latest, and had rushed up to give her a hug as soon as she'd seen her at the show that morning. Hearing Tallulah going on about entering the Cup, Poppy winked at Alice, then headed on towards the warm-up area. But Tallulah caught sight of her rival and, mid-sentence, kicked Diamond Starr on, leaving Alice hanging as she trotted nearer to Poppy.

Alice shook her head and turned her attention back to the ring. A portly judge waved and called over to her and the group of ponies and horses waiting in a group nearby.

"Can we have all entries for the 'Pony With the Shiniest Coat' please!"

"We are going to have so much fun, I promise!" Rosie beamed, getting excited as they headed in. "And anyway, it's about time we entered something that me and Dancer actually have a chance of winning!"

"Okay, come on then, let's go for it!" Charlie laughed. Pirate jigged along behind Dancer. The mare's strawberry roan coat gleamed in the sun, after Rosie had spent ages polishing it that morning. Alice rode in behind them with Mia, and stood Scout squarely for a moment. The judge stepped along the line. She admired the variety of ponies in front of her then asked everyone to walk around the ring while she contemplated her decision.

Rosie was called in at the front of the line by the judge, winning her first red rosette of the summer. Over the moon, Rosie took off on the slowest ever lap of honour waving one hand wildly, and whooping as Charlie and Mia cheered her on. Alice laughed, patting her pony's sturdy, solid neck. She felt as delighted as Rosie as she stood in the ring with her three best friends, feeling like the luckiest girl in the universe. Alice leaned down and kissed Scout's neck, hugging him tightly. She knew now that there could be no more secrets about his past. And while she might not know yet what her grey pony's future would hold, one thing was certain – it would always be with her.

Alice's Guide to the Perfect Jumping Position

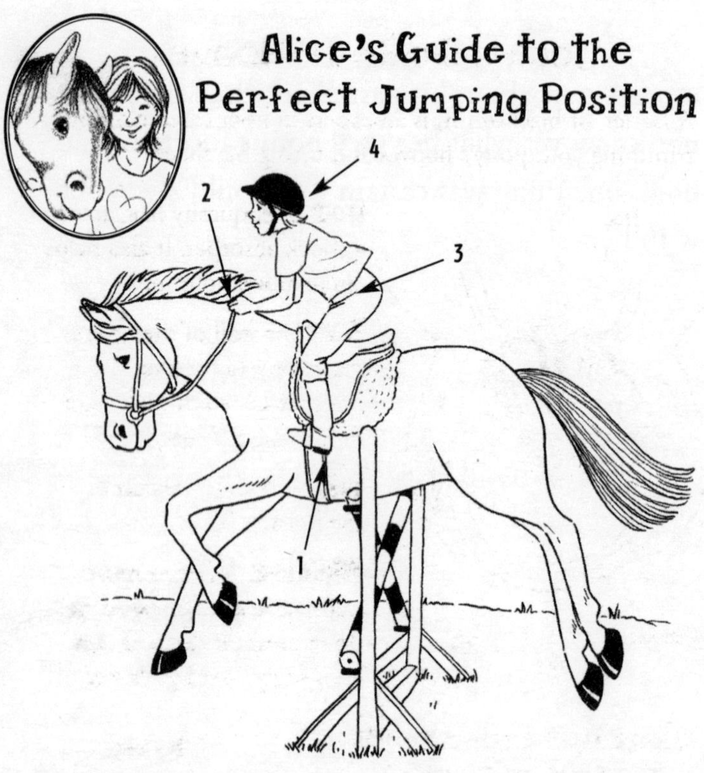

1 Keep the weight in your heels. This will help you keep your lower leg still and make you secure in the saddle.

2 Soften your hands in the last stride and let them follow the movement of your pony's head. This will allow him to stretch his neck over the fence.

3 Fold from your hips when your pony jumps. Don't fold before this, or you'll put more weight onto his shoulders just when he's trying to lift them off the ground!

4 Keep your head up and look where you're going.

Jock's Guide to Hooves

A farrier, or blacksmith, is an expert in hoof care, including trimming your pony's hooves and fitting his shoes.

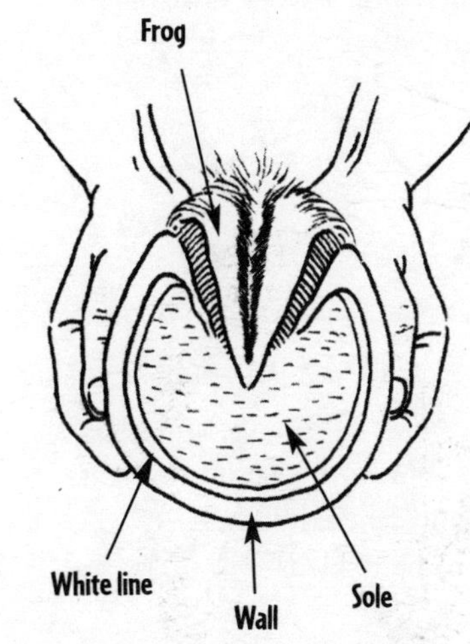

Frog: The squashy frog acts as a shock absorber. It also helps circulation and grip.

Wall: The wall of the hoof is insensitive (a bit like fingernails), so this is where horseshoe nails go.

Sole: The sensitive part of the hoof.

White line: A farrier must make sure the horseshoe nails don't press on this – if they do a pony could go lame.

Signs that a pony needs the farrier to visit:

- Clenches (the ends of the nail which you can see on the hoof wall) become raised.
- The shoe gets worn and thin.
- The shoe becomes loose (it makes a shallow sort of noise on roads), or falls off!

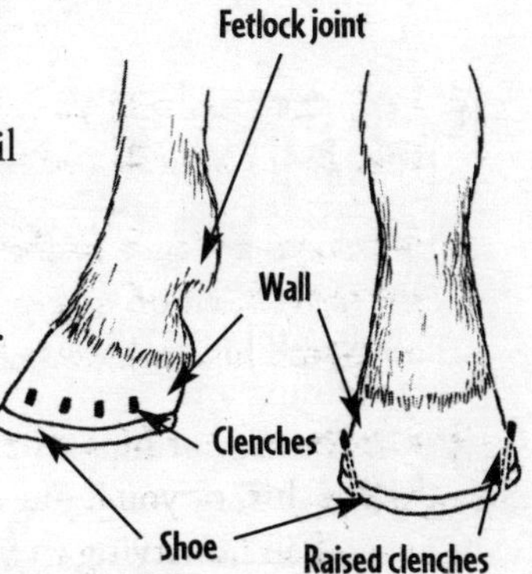

Did you know?

Some racehorses wear glued-on shoes when they race!

How to Tell if You and Your Pony are Best Friends

Does your pony:

- come over to see you when you visit him in the paddock?

- rest his muzzle on your shoulder?

- look after you when you're riding and slow down if you're in danger of sliding off?

Do you:

- take ages grooming your pony, just so you can spend lots of time with him?

- know his favourite treats and where he likes to be tickled?

- spend every spare second with him (although you make sure he has pony time on his own and with his friends, too)?

Yes to any of these? Then you and your pony are BPFFs! (Best Pony Friends Forever!)